"Fragoza's prose, a switchblade of a magical glow, cauterizes as it cuts. In a setting of barren citrus trees, poison-filled balloons, and stuccos haunted by the menace of the past, *Eat the Mouth That Feeds You* reinvents the sunny noir."

—**Salvador Plascencia**, author of *The People of Paper*

"I felt this collection deep in my bones. Like the Chicanx women whose voices she centers, Carribean Fragoza's writing doesn't flinch. It is sharp and dream-like, tender-hearted and brutal, carved from the violence and resilience of generations past and present."

—**Natalia Sylvester**, author of *Everyone Knows You Go Home*

"Carribean Fragoza's writing is passionate and precise... gorgeously goth."

—**Yxta Maya Murray**, *Poets and Writers Magazine*

"Carribean Fragoza goes deep. This book makes central the lives of women, whether sourced locally or rooted in Mexico, whether alive or dead to the world, surrealistic or hyperrealistic, in the flesh or as spirits centuries old. This is storytelling that astonishes, passing through industrialized lives of women like gamma rays or cosmic rays—and I was not only astonished, I was moved. Kafka said, 'A book must be an axe for the frozen sea that is within us.' Be careful how you heft this book—it's sharp as obsidian, this axe."

—**Sesshu Foster**, author of *Atomik Aztex*

EAT THE MOUTH THAT FEEDS YOU

EAT
THE
MOUTH
THAT
FEEDS
YOU

CARRIBEAN FRAGOZA

CITY LIGHTS BOOKS

Cover photograph: Graciela Iturbide, Untitled, Chalmita, México, 1982

Cover design by em dash

ISBN: 978-0-87286-833-5

Library of Congress Cataloging-in-Publication Data

Names: Fragoza, Carribean, author.
Title: Eat the mouth that feeds you / by Carribean Fragoza.
Description: San Francisco : City Lights Books, 2020.
Identifiers: LCCN 2020013754 | ISBN 9780872868335 (trade paperback)
Subjects: LCSH: Latin Americans—United States—Fiction. | Hispanic
    American women—Fiction. | Mexican-American Border Region—Fiction.
Classification: LCC PS3606.R348 A6 2020 | DDC 813/.6—dc23
LC record available at https://lccn.loc.gov/2020013754

City Lights Books are published at the City Lights Bookstore
261 Columbus Avenue, San Francisco, CA 94133
www.citylights.com

CONTENTS

For Romeo, Aura, and Camila

EAT THE MOUTH THAT FEEDS YOU

LUMBERJACK MOM

~~~~~

THAT SPRING, WHEN the dormant roots and seeds started sprouting and our father stopped coming home, our mother took to the backyard with fervent urgency. Overnight, it seemed, vegetation had burst through the cracks, split the tile and cement, broken through the clay pots and tin cans. Grass spilled over the hedges with a despicable gusto. One morning, my brother and I woke up to find our breakfast already cold on the kitchen counter and our mother at work in the backyard, crawling on her hands and knees, clawing out odd weeds with tiny flowers we'd never seen before that now burgeoned in tenacious clusters throughout the lawn. She dedicated hours to these new invaders, ripping them out from the grass like clumps of hair. Fistfuls of roots dangling dirt and squirming worms like freshly torn scalps still steaming. Our mother's face sweated and twisted under the sun. We watched her silently from the bathroom window, heads butted together. We heard our sister call out from another window, Mom are you okay? Yes, *mija*. It's just hot, she answered, wiping the sweat with the back of her bare hand.

The next day, we noticed she'd pulled out some gardening tools, small hoes and some shears that she sharpened with a rock.

We recognized the hand-size, volcanic slab from our grandmother's house in Guadalajara, from before she passed away. One of her prized possessions, our grandmother had used it to sharpen her knives and shears, sitting alone and in silence at the head of the table. My brother and I would sit in front of the TV and pretend not to watch her. She'd then retreat into the kitchen with her knives to perform mysterious domestic acts.

Our mother used her freshly sharpened tools to cut up the thick roots of unidentified plants that seemed to be waiting for the right time to reveal themselves. She wasn't going to give them a chance. Eventually, we noticed that her favorite tool was a set of narrow-nosed pliers that she'd stab into the ground to extract even the most reluctant roots. She'd have to pull very hard, sometimes using both hands and the weight of her small body. Often it was the thin, spidery roots that were the most persistent and dug themselves in the deepest. Our mother, however, was very thorough, for any remnant would have sabotaged everything.

She also found tiny insects chewing at the leaves of potted plants that she'd grown from cuttings or from seeds she'd sprouted herself. She trimmed not only these contaminated leaves, but also the ones she suspected would soon become infected. At first she snipped gently at the herbs, only removing the diseased tops of the *hierbabuena* or oregano. Eventually, she cut them down to stubby brown stems, but left those roots intact.

As the days passed, we watched her rove through the garden, flower bed to flower bed, potted plant to potted plant, and then cycle back methodically to rip out the invasive flower clusters that resurfaced in the grass. When she arrived at the lime tree's jagged shadow, she immediately got up off her hands and knees. I thought she might have hunched after spending so much time curled over the ground or that she might need to steady her head if it was spinning with blood having been bent low beneath the sun. But she stood straight up before the lime tree as if measuring her height against it. She seemed taller than usual, as if she had height stored inside of her for certain occasions.

That night at supper, my siblings and I watched her swallow down a large glass of water with hardly a breath. And then she announced that she wanted to cut down the lime tree. My brother and sister and I looked at each other in silence. Although she'd never outright said so, we knew she'd wanted to cut it down for some time now. The tree is useless if it doesn't produce limes, she stated bluntly. And that, she pointed out, was our father's fault.

When we were very young, my parents had lovingly smuggled the seeds in their luggage from Mexico. They wrapped them in embroidered, perfumed handkerchiefs that they carefully packed into plastic baggies, rolled into socks and then stuffed into tennis shoes. They'd even planted a decoy in their suitcase so that when the customs people pulled out our candied fruits and held up the sugared rolls to toss them ceremoniously in a trash bin, we feigned disappointment. Together, bound by complicity, we silently relished our secret accomplishment, and held warmly in our hearts the knowledge of those protected little seeds that were on their way to starting a new generation. Just like us.

Together, we watched the tree grow. We talked to it as one might talk to a baby, using sweet gibberish and tickling its leaves. We'd tell it what a lovely little tree it was, oh what a beautiful little tree growing so big so big now, bigger every day look at you, drink your water, stretch toward the sun, *ay qué bonito limoncito*. We celebrated every one of its lime tree milestones, its first tender branch and its first flower. Its first lime was observed carefully and treasured. How we loved its sour fruit. She had loved it too.

Over time we allowed the tree to grow at its own whim, not having the heart to cut off a single one of its beloved leaves or branches. However, instead of growing juicy limes that ripened fully and dropped to the green grass for us to gather, it produced many tiny, hard limes that it guarded with a web of knotted branches and vicious thorns. The fruit would ripen deep within the foliage and finally drop to rot on the ground. The interior growth was so dense and low that we could no longer reach under it to rescue the limes. The shade spoiled the ground, and the lime acid spoiled it too. Most trees that spoil their own ground, roots deprived of essential nutrients, gradually suffocate themselves. Yet this one continued to grow, and we accepted it, cruel thorns and all.

Several years ago, our father made his last attempt at landscaping. My mother had asked him to prune the tree, said that it had been choking itself with its own gnarled branches. The tree needed maintenance and care like any other living being, my mother said to my father. He knew where she was headed with this, so he grabbed a machete from the garage and began chopping. He left the tree entirely bereft of its flowers, fruit and foliage, sparing only a large chewed-up grey bulk of thorny twigs and branches attached to its short trunk. It looked like a lopsided brain that had been cut up but remained alive, sputtering splintered thoughts. We wept for days, including our mother, and our father didn't come home until we shut up. Our poor tree. After several seasons, it eventually recovered its green leaves and grew back its barbed branches, and it even began to flower, but refused to give fruit altogether.

My siblings and I continued to watch the lime tree for signs. We studied the flower buds, careful not to disturb the fragile petals. We also refused to trim it, even though we knew, as we always had, that we should for the good of the tree. We loved it, perhaps as much as we loved each other, but didn't know how to care for it.

Since then, our mother had avoided the tree. She had blocked it from her field of vision, until now. Sitting at the dinner table, my brother and I said nothing in response to my mother's idea. However, we saw that our sister was carefully sifting through something in her mind. It shifted quietly in her head, trickling a little in one direction then another, moving it in a subtle bob that was neither a nod nor a shake. Through the silence, our mother's thoughts seemed to have moved on to a different subject as she finished off her meal in a few large bites and stood up to gather the dishes from the table. As she disappeared into the kitchen, we could still hear her chewing, crunching on her char-edged tortilla. I thought for an instant of her strong teeth, large for her small thin-lipped mouth. None of us had inherited teeth like that.

After several days, when she had finished tearing bald spots into the lawn and taming the hedges, at least for a while, she noticed all of the crap we'd put out in the yard over the years and forgotten about. Mostly defunct furniture we never got around to throwing away. She turned her instinct to an old chest of drawers we'd long abandoned in the far end of the yard, where it was now rotting. From our usual window, my brother and I watched her break it up with her bare hands. A family of cats ran out, the kittens chasing after their mother. She pushed the chest over on its side like a small whale carcass and pulled on the panels with the weight of her body. She tore out small rusted nails and staples that once held the pieces together. We could hear her grunt as she worked, clenching her teeth, the bone of her jaw gleaming. The veins in her forearms and hands bulged as she pulled and snapped off the rotting boards.

At dinnertime, we watched her bandaged fingers scoop food from her plate with bits of tortilla. Without looking at us, she said, I've been thinking about getting rid of some of the old furniture in the house. My brother and I were overjoyed, relieved. Our sister's head bobbed excitedly. There was plenty of old, not to mention ugly, furniture we'd insisted on getting rid of for ages. Most of it was furniture my parents bought on layaway when we were still babies. By now, their emotional value had worn out. Their laminated surfaces blistered and peeled, revealing the cheap particleboard underneath.

The next day, our mother showed us a new pile of what used to be a bookshelf. The following day, a sewing table. Throughout the week, some old chairs, an entertainment center, a lazy boy. She found a rusty saw among the tools our father had abandoned in the garage. She sawed into the legs of various upright pieces, then broke them down into smaller pieces, which she arranged into tall piles in the middle of the yard. As the days grew longer, she'd work later through the afternoon and the piles got larger. My siblings and I came out to the yard to admire them at the end of each day. At dusk, our sister hugged our mother until it grew dark, while my brother and I filled the trash bin with debris. We smiled too, but started to think that maybe she'd cut up enough furniture. We didn't want her to start chopping the stuff that we actually liked and needed.

It occurred to us, my brother and me, that our mother had demonstrated such natural chopping skills, that perhaps she could make an excellent lumberjack. We imagined her out in the woods somewhere marching with great determination, every part of her body radiating strength as she swung her ax at redwoods that were no match for her. With a single blow she'd splinter the entire thing into perfect logs that would land in neatly arranged cabins, their small windows somehow already curtained. Our mother, smiling sweated gold.

We decided to surprise her with a new ax and a small pile of neat logs. We installed one strong stump in the yard to hold the blocks, take the blows and hacks. She went at it immediately with remarkable precision and grace, like a dancer slicing each log down the middle. It was a beautiful thing to watch. She held that ax as naturally as if it were the hairbrush she'd used, until recently, to brush her hair out of a braid while she waited for our father late into the night. She'd brush and brush until her long hair gleamed like cascading water or the grain of polished wood.

Now that her wait was over, she just split logs most of the afternoon, one after the other in clean strokes. In the evenings she oiled her calloused hands before walking off to bed without saying goodnight.

Every morning we'd find our mother in the yard, chopping away at logs or pausing to scan the yard for returning weeds. She spent most of her time outdoors, coming inside only to use the restroom, drink some water and prepare her usual tortilla thinly slathered with beans and a bite of raw green chile. My siblings and I were also on the bean-tortilla diet. Following her brief meal, without a pause, she'd wipe her hands on her clothes and reach out again for the ax. My brother and I were pleased by her focus and commitment, but started to wonder what would come next.

To break the monotony of watching this daily routine through the bathroom window, we started playing checkers in the bathtub. We waited for an idea to come to us about what to do next as we listened to the sound of wood cracking beneath a neatly sharpened blade. One day, the sound of screams shook us from our pensive game. We ran outside to find her axing through the weathered boards of our backyard fence. Our sister stood by, watching with crossed arms. The neighbors stood frozen in shock over their vegetable patch as my mother shredded the old wood fence. They were nice people. They often left grocery bags filled with freshly picked oranges, sometimes odd fruits we didn't have names for, hanging on our side of the fence. Usually they smiled and waved at us from their back porch. Today they gripped onions to their hearts, shouted at us in their language. She remained focused on the fence even while my brother tore the ax from her white knuckles and I held her tightly against my body with all of my strength. I could feel her heavy breath pushing through her small rib cage. I expected to feel her heart whipping its wings against her ribs like a parakeet shaken in its cage. Instead, inside I felt a large furry animal balled up, breathing slow but strong. It waited patiently to break out.

We knew that she was ready for more than mere log splitting. My brother and I deliberated while our mother rested in the dark living room, our sister watching her intently. By dinnertime, we had a plan. We proposed an excursion to a nearby mountain to cut down her first tree, after which, we promised to treat her to dinner at her favorite Italian restaurant. Another silence spread over the dinner table. Our sister peered at our mom from the bottom of the glass of water she'd long finished drinking. After a minute or two, our mother stopped glaring through the blinds at something in the yard and seemed to be considering our proposal. Finally, she nodded, tight-lipped. We accepted that as a gesture of approval and even perhaps determination. We felt encouraged. Things were going to move forward.

The following Saturday morning, we wrapped up her ax in an old crocheted blanket we found in the garage. It used to be our baby blanket, but for this occasion, we'd pulled it out of the black trash bag where my mother had stored it. We all packed into the car and drove up the nearest mountain until we found enough trees to call it a woods.

My brother and I had printed out instructions from the Internet for beginner lumberjacks. Apparently, selecting a proper tree for your experience level and body type was essential. We fumbled with the instructions while our mom and sister opened the trunk and carefully pulled out the ax, still wrapped in its blanket. It seemed heavier here in the woods, its steel duller but somehow more dangerous, and its wooden handle felt like it might blister one's hands more easily. Something about the air here made everything more so.

We scouted around for a proper tree, calling back to our mom to put on her new gloves and get ready. My brother and I disagreed and then agreed on a tree. We chose a medium-size tree that seemed to be drying up. It looked ashy all over, and we could see some dusty spiderwebs up in its branches. The bark flaked off easily in thick scabs against our palms.

My brother and I shuffled through the crumpled printouts. There were sections about posture and handling the ax and how to strike your tree at just the right angle. It seemed there was a right way and a wrong way to cut down a tree. Our eyes glazed over the italicized and underlined phrases, the little diagrams of people and trees with green check marks next to them for Yes, red circles and slashes for No. We just wanted our mom to get right to it. Cutting trees is a timeless practice, we figured. Didn't we all cut trees at some point to build our civilizations? It must be the kind of thing you get the hang of once you get going. Although we briefly talked about having our mom use a hard hat or some kind of helmet, we realized that we hadn't brought one along, so that ended that conversation. We decided not to read the rest of the instructions.

When we returned, our mother leaned against the car eating sandwiches out of paper napkins with my sister. She offered us the ones she'd packed for us, but we told her it was time to get to work on that tree we'd picked out for her. She pulled on the new gloves and flexed her fingers to break in the tough leather. She picked up the ax awkwardly, without a hint of the grace we'd witnessed days earlier. When we arrived at the tree, she stopped. She seemed to not know what to do. Neither did we. We tried to encourage her. Try it out, just hit it and it'll come! You'll figure it out! You can do it!

She tried swinging the ax but had a hard time raising it over her shoulder. Her wrists kept getting twisted up. She couldn't even figure out how to stand and kept shifting and switching her feet around. Finally, she swung and the blade hit the flaky trunk. A few bark chips flew off. She swung and hit it again with a thud and some dust fell from the spider webs onto my sister's hair. My sister is terrified of spiders.

My brother and I realized something. Chopping down a tree in the woods is completely different from chopping up furniture or logs in the yard. Nothing was happening.

Our mother dropped the ax onto the pine needles covering the forest floor. She didn't want to do it. Her heart wasn't in it. It was more difficult than we all expected. And besides, she said, the tree, although it was dying, deserved to die with dignity on its own. Let's just leave it alone. Just leave it alone and let it die, she said softly.

My brother and I stared at the ax on the ground. I ran to it, panicked that already it might be rusting and then all hope would be lost. Our mother dropped to the foot of the tree and buried her face in our sister's arms.

After that, our mother insisted on staying indoors. She picked up the crochet needle my grandmother had left her, complete with an unfinished doily still attached to the spool of thread. My mother's siblings had found the crocheted thing at the base of our grandmother's armchair shortly after she passed away, and somehow figured that my mother should have it, though she had never crocheted. Nonetheless, she'd kept it at the base of her own seat on the couch. We watched her pick up the doily and needle. She held it in her hands and laid it on her lap before throwing it back to the floor, and remained still and silent until it became dark.

My brother and I wished she would pick up the ax again. We bought a fresh pile of logs and even collected some old furniture from the neighbors, hoping to entice her back to chopping. We rubbed the rust out of the steel and even oiled the wooden handle. We laid it out on a pretty gingham cloth next to a pitcher of cold lemonade on the kitchen table though she hardly made her way to the kitchen at all now. If only we could get her started again, we could figure out what to do next.

She remained in the living room for three days.

On the fourth day, my brother and I went out to collect more furniture discarded along the curb. We weren't ready to give up on our mother. We began arranging the pieces around the front and backyard. We placed them by the front door and near windows where she might catch sight of them. There was one particularly attractive small log about the size of a meaty arm that we even left out on a coffee table in the living room.

When we returned from one of our excursions, we noticed a trail of splinters, long shreds of wood. The small tables we'd left in the front yard had been pulverized. We were excited. We looked at each other eagerly. Finally! Our mother, we were going to have our mother back. We'd figured things out. We were going to make the best of it.

We followed the trail of debris to the backyard. We followed the sound of her ax. It sounded different than wooden logs or particle board or panels of cherrywood or anything like that. Our sister stood solemnly at the gate to the yard and did not look at us.

We found our mother chopping through a tangle of branches. Her arms were gashed by the long thorns, as if they'd been fighting back for their lives. Her face was also covered in a web of thin scratches, but they were hardly visible against her darkly tanned face. The scratches were lined with tiny beads of black blood that shone like unblinking eyes in the sun.

The lime tree, our little lime tree. We were aghast. She had chopped it down. She chopped our lime tree down to brambles. She'd slashed off all of the leafy branches without regard for the countless white blossoms, heavy with pollen and bees. The yard was littered with tender leaves, their young flesh brilliantly green against the coarse dry grass. The blossom scent was sweet in the dense air. She'd cut through the tree's gnarled underbrush, which was piled waist-high all around her. She stood at the center of a ring of thorns with the amputated limbs strewn at her feet. Through the underbrush, we could see that the limbs had been healthy and green at their core. They were covered not in scabby bark, but in a thin skin that would break easily even with the lightest fingernail scratch. We remembered how vulnerable the tree always felt to us.

Oblivious to us, our mother continued chopping the remaining branches with greater ease and expertise than we had ever witnessed before. Finally, she arrived at its naked trunk that stood alone among the brambles that now filled most of the yard. We could not reach our mother without crossing this field of thorns. Our mother, ax in hand, and the tree trunk, alone, guarded by this destruction.

We cried out, "No!" Not our tree, not our little lime tree, but our shrieks awakened her from her dizzy reverie, and then, as if in reflex, she swung the ax into the tree's body, piercing it halfway with the blow. And without pause, she swung again a final time, leaving but a thin ligament of green fiber attached at the base of the tree's neck. Without breathing, we watched our mother drop the ax over the bed of thorns and grip the trunk's limp fiber with both hands. She wrenched it free with one long grunt that became a scream at the end. It shook the wild parrots out of the neighboring trees, and all we could do was watch them flap away as her scream dissipated into the hot, colorless sky. And the air became very still and unusually quiet. Except for my mother's breath, which came in long draughts, in and out like a strong tide.

THE VICIOUS LADIES

~~~~~~

AT THE FAR end of the backyard, nestled in overgrown summer grass, the girls huddled around their private nitrous oxide tank. One at a time, they collapsed into the waiting arms of the other Ladies. The more experienced ones knew when to pull the colored balloon from their painted lips. A few seconds longer and a girl could have a much harder fall, like the stupid boys over there who mostly toppled over, smacking their teeth against the concrete patio, drooling and bleeding onto their mom-ironed shirts. The Vicious Ladies knew better and they took care of each other. Partying, they'd learned, was not only their business, it was also a way of life and they were going to do it right.

It was like watching a clandestine baptism. The girls faithfully dropped their bodies into the invisible waters that would make them new. And the noz did. Each emerged from their trip smiling, like they'd all seen some variation of a god that was gentle and kind and sometimes very funny.

Since we started bringing the noz, the parties are even more unbearable. From my seat on a plastic milk crate next to the empty beer cans and stench of dog urine, I can't stop watching the kids suck on balloons, and roll their eyes back into their heads and open their mouths like they're about to speak in tongues. They don't know that this god they experience has a name. It's called Samira. And this is all part of Samira's plan that has only begun to unfold, exactly as she expects it to. Her genius evades and disgusts me. And I hate all of them. I hate the Vicious Ladies.

The older Vicious Ladies, too old for nitrous oxide, were getting down. They bounced their fat *chichis* and asses all over the place to whatever monotonous beats the DJ played. The homies mostly stood around hugging their beers and looking for thongs through the daisy dukes. A few early drinkers waddled their way onto the dance floor and swayed in their oversize pants, circling the buoyant Ladies as closely as they could. Their dumb drunken smiles made me feel sorry for them. These guys had no clue what they were dealing with. One bad move and any of these Ladies could disembowel them, no problem. Bunch of assholes. They paid money to party—after all, this was a Vicious Ladies party.

This is what I've come home to.

The same old shit. Except worse. Older and shittier. Rebecca is the same slut as always, but with blonder hair and more stretch marks. She rubs her ass, packed all tight into a tiny white miniskirt, up against a boy young enough to be her son. Watch him get a hard-on for that saggy piece of Rebecca ass. They are too old to be doing this. *I* am too old to be doing this.

But they don't care what I think. The Vicious Ladies took me in like an adopted little sister. A lost puppy they felt sorry for and ended up loving. It doesn't matter that I hate them all. Samira finds my disgust endearing, which only fuels my hatred even more. It's a terrible cycle.

When the Ladies pull up in front of my house, I have no choice. I have to make a quick exit before one of them gets out of the car and my mother can catch a good look at them. As it is, from inside the car, their AquaNet-teased bangs form an aura of hair suspicious enough to make my mother scowl through the kitchen curtains. When she asks *"¿Adónde vas?"* in that tone of voice of hers from the couch, I have to hurry up and make up a new baptism or *quinceañera* party that I'm late to before I walk out the door. When she's too insistent I have to slam the door extra hard.

I don't know which is worse, my mother pacing around in the house like a caged parrot or the Ladies waiting for me like a car full of clown buzzards. I often think about escaping both, running into the shadows of the neighbors' yards, hurtling over fences from one lawn to another until…well, I don't know what. That's part of the problem, I guess. I wouldn't know what I'd be running toward.

I rush to the curb and leap into the Ladies' packed Honda before anyone can see. I make sure to slump low in the back seat before we peel away with a screech like we're a pile of witches in a hurry.

Every time, I start out by convincing myself it might not be so bad. Lately, I have to try harder. Tonight, I even dressed up, squeezed into a pair of tight jeans and a sexy tank top. Gel-slicked my hair into a shiny ponytail. When the DJ got going I even tried dancing out there on the patio with all the other *nalgonas*. I tried to feel the synthie rhythm in my blood, the thumping beats in my bones, fill my brain with flashing colored lights, cloud my eyes with fog. I wanted to forget about the balloon girls giggling in the grass.

Only a month ago, this time, I was drinking pots of coffee and agonizing over all-nighter papers like my life depended on the defense of a thesis. So long as I was reading the books, the essays and the articles, I knew what to do. Now the objective was to stop thinking altogether and find the urge to move with a beat. To simply go with the flow because any hypothesis I could possibly come up with would be worthless.

Defeat weighed on my entire being and made for bad dancing. I felt my limbs stiffen, falling out of sync with the music and everything around me. I stood paralyzed in the middle of the patio among a swarm of bobbing bodies in the froth of a fog machine cloud.

I dragged myself out toward the street and perched my feet over the curb, staring down at the gutter. I needed a breath of air, a suggestion of black sky, something resembling peace.

The trees cooled the rosebushes and mint leaves. Even shadows rested.

I inhaled the sweet air when that familiar white Town Car with tinted windows rolled silently from behind and stopped beside me. The engine's heat rose up my legs and car exhaust invaded my nostrils. I knew that on the other side of the windows was Samira. Of course, Samira.

"Where you going, girl?" Her voice cut through the darkness.

This was no pleasure visit. Samira was here to check up on business. She stepped out of the car with jaguar-like grace, her smile radiating and her eyes shining like obsidian blades.

"Why so lonely?" she said, leaning to kiss me, her gold-hoop earring brushing against my cheek.

I shrugged, staring at the asphalt to avoid her face.

"Sounds like it's bumping in there."

I didn't answer. I could feel her inspecting me.

"C'mere *mija*, I wanna show you something," she said, leading me into the white leather cocoon of her car's back seat, a veritable office on wheels. She had an arrangement of notepads, calculators, colored pens, a stack of color-coded binders, and clipboards covered in neatly columned spreadsheets. Pages and pages of numbers warbled off a language that I didn't understand but found oddly comforting.

The first time Samira told me about the noz, I didn't know what she was talking about. "Nitrous oxide? What the hell are you supposed to do with that? We're gonna gas kids?"

"Noz is harmless," she assured me. "It's like laughing gas but you inhale it from a balloon. Makes you feel good all over, but just for a few seconds. It's a quick high. Then it's over and the kids line up to buy another."

I imagined kids flopping around the floor like dying fish, vomiting all over the place from their gaping mouths. I had Fox News Undercover on replay, police raiding the house and kids scattering like *cucarachas*, Samira and I in handcuffs getting shoved into the police car. My mom watching everything on the eleven o'clock news. We look ten pounds fatter on TV.

I knew we already made plenty at the door and with the alcohol. Even the weed, which Samira didn't sell directly—she found a way to take her cut anyway. With Samira, all of the Vicious Ladies took their cut.

"It's harmless," she repeated, trying to assuage me. I knew this was not a conversation. Samira was showing me what was coming.

"You and I are Vicious Ladies. Partying is our business and, more importantly, a way of life. It's us, not their mothers, who teach the young ones to respect each other and their elders. We teach them how to be women. When to close their legs and when to open them. We teach them how to stand in front of anyone and look them in the eye with a straight face. We teach our girls how to defend themselves and take what's theirs because no one else will."

Sure enough, Samira's got it all under control. The numbers on the spreadsheets were evidence that things were going better than I could have imagined. But not Samira. Nothing surprises her because nothing is outside of her calculations. The DJs, the equipment, the door guys, the flyers, the dancers, the alcohol, the weed, the noz, and, of course, us—the Vicious Ladies—all part of a serious, thriving business. Legitimate or not, legal or not, this hustle was real. What else were we gonna do? Work fast food or retail for shit money and dick bosses?

I surrendered myself to the soft leather. Samira laid it out simply like a nice little math equation with proofs. This was not the life I had imagined for myself at all. But the truth is, I couldn't really imagine anything else.

WALKING GETS DESPERATE. Standing at corners waiting for lights is the worst, which is why I usually ride the old dirt bike my brother abandoned and I adopted as my own. I found it in the garage leaned up against all the shit my father left behind, too.

After a long ride around the neighborhood, back in the cool shade of the garage, I can be alone to rest, to think. My books are all stacked up in about a dozen boxes against the back wall. I pull them out by their spines like small animals that I love. I inspect each one, paging through them, petting the paper, running my finger over the words like coaxing out the little *nagual* animal that is mine to travel, Castañeda-style, way the fuck somewhere else, to another universe.

In the first days of summer, I'd go into the house and look through the stack of old framed photos and award plaques from grade school. They were covered in dust next to dozens of smashed spiders. Before long my mother would start moaning about something I didn't want to hear, like, "*Mija* what are you doing? What are you gonna do with your life? What are you going to be?"

Like what I do and who I am is not enough. Like there's gotta be some payoff or a whole different, marvelous world at the other end of this tunnel—one she's been expecting this whole time. Well, here I am, on the other side, and there is nothing, just my feet skidding on blank air like Wile E. Coyote. The trick is to keep running across the void like you don't know there's nothing there.

When I look at her, I can see my mother moonwalking in place inside her own personal tunnel, going nowhere. Suspecting the edge and the unknown beyond, she will never arrive. And I realize I'm all on my own to figure things out. I gotta keep going.

Except for Samira, I'm really on my own.

My mother's aches spread all through her body and she started spending more time in bed, so she went to Mexico with her sisters to get treatment. The pills she was taking weren't doing anything except make her vomit all day. And since I haven't really been around much to help, she decided to try her luck with the prayer breathers and *hierberos*. They have pretty potent plants down there. Here all we've got is palm trees that are good for nothing and some damn persistent weeds that keep pushing up through land that's like a pummeled parking lot. I don't blame my mother for leaving. She needs to be in a more nurturing environment.

THE FIRST VICIOUS Lady I knew was Patricia. No one would believe it now, but she was in algebra class our seventh grade year, with me and all the other dorks and nerds. A few weeks into our first semester, I watched her slip into a seat across the room and thought, Oh God, what is *she* doing here. She sat, smiling quietly to herself, surrounded by boys shoving one another for their turn to tell her another stupid joke. They said anything, no matter how stupid, to get her to laugh. Perfectly smart boys acting like dumbasses. Her lips were a dark, nearly black, burgundy. The boys were desperate to see the velvety curtain of her lips part. Her eyes, rimmed in black charcoal, were always laughing too. But it was her huge breasts that at thirteen years of age eclipsed everyone and everything. Their soft mass quivered gently with every giggle with which she generously awarded their ridiculous efforts.

For all I cared, she could keep her big obstructive tits. I kept waiting for those burgundy lips to say something that would reveal her fraudulent presence in Algebra I for overachieving seventh graders.

But Patricia didn't have to say a thing. Whenever the teacher asked her to do a math problem on the blackboard she knew exactly what to do. She rose from her seat, magnetizing every eyeball. Her ringed fingers expertly held a piece of chalk and laid out a white map that dribbled perfectly down the green chalkboard. Math was nothing to her. Every movement was simple and clear, unlike my own desperate markings that scrawled over themselves and smudged into threatening, murky clouds.

Of course, our teacher assigned Patty as my math buddy. Before long, I realized the logic of the pairing. Patty was going to help me keep up in class, which she did with great ease and patience. I resented this deeply. While I wrestled with unwieldy math equations, she chatted away about boys, family, and the

Vicious Ladies as if she'd known me forever. She'd make some brief edits on my sheet, realigning my toppling stacks of numbers and confide to me, "I know one day you're going to be famous. I know it. You're all smart and shit, get good grades, think for yourself. But if anyone fucks with you, ever, we've got your back."

How could she talk like that? I could not imagine saying such touchy-feely things to anyone. That easy confidence was the kind I imagined was shared between people who go way back, survived famine or war together. This was middle school.

I inspected my worksheet with her adjustments. I always got the variables wrong, lost track of the positives and the negatives, strayed from the columns and mixed up the numbers.

"Look," Patty said, "all you gotta do is hang with us. Just chill there, you don't even have to do a thing. Just hang with us."

But in the years that followed, and through the end of high school, I did my best to keep as far away from the Vicious Ladies as I could. Despite their misshapen feelings of solidarity, I wanted to have nothing to do with them. When the pack of girls rolled through campus, as they always did, keeping close vigilance over an invisible territory they believed they claimed, I made sure to stay on the exact diametric opposite end of their orbit. But nothing I did or didn't do seemed to bother them. Not even when I said no to them. They simply ignored me and absorbed me into their little galaxy, though I kept myself apart like a renegade space rock, hanging as far as I could on the outer edges of their ring.

23

THERE WAS NO way of knowing how old Samira was. When I first saw her standing and waiting by the fence around the school field, she seemed old, yet ageless.

"That's her," Patty said to me in a low voice. I was only twelve years old but already I knew we were walking toward a terrible fate. Mine in particular. I felt something heavy shift at the bottom of my belly. My backpack felt heavy too. We were walking down the sidewalk toward Samira. To be accurate, I was walking to the liquor store on the corner to buy a nice cold popsicle because I was on my long sweaty way home. I had cartoons to watch and homework to do. I was *not* walking to Samira. But like always, she was inescapably in the way.

As we got closer, more girls gathered around Samira, solidifying the circle one girl at a time. Girls trickled down the street, others drifted across the field and squeezed through an opening snipped through the chain link fence.

"Patty, I gotta go home," I said, but she was used to my whining. She linked her arm through mine, and pulled me along anyway. "Don't worry, we're just going to see what's up." The dread in my belly persisted. I knew that "seeing what's up" could mean anything. It could come to mean something entirely different from what you had intended. It was not up to you to control "what's up." "What's up" might never end.

We arrived at the crowd and waited like everyone else. There was something sparking in the moist air among the girls, laughing and snapping sharp and shiny things. I recognized Patricia's friends, the Vicious Ladies.

In this crowd, I was the blunt one standing cold and reluctant. I wanted to go home. I thought about the latest book I'd checked out from the library. I wanted to hide with it in a corner of my house so I could breathe through this book—a portal—the right kind of air from a different atmosphere, where I was sure

I belonged. I wanted to be left alone. Instead, I stayed close to Patty.

There were several dozen girls, mostly ones that I had never seen before. Although I could not see Samira, I could sense her in the middle of everything.

Nadine's heart-shaped smiling face and black cherry lips pushed through the crowd at us. "Patty! Here, here." She was her best friend. They called her Tear Drop because of the small scar she had below the corner of her right eye. She handed us colorful glossy cards and nudged tightly against Patty's side. Then the party flyers came darting and drifting from overhead. Hands reached for the color-saturated flyers flashing all around. The closest thing I knew to snow besides Easter egg confetti. Through the multicolored snow I caught a glimpse of Samira's black smile and her knowing eyes.

I was swallowed into their circle of perfumed bodies, the jangle of gold hoops and glow-in-the dark jewelry. The more I tried to push myself out, the closer Samira got. The Vicious Ladies closed in around me, and in the center, it was always Samira. She generated her own gravitational pull, like a black hole. She was a star that had imploded into itself and was the very substance of the void, made of nothing but the relentless suck of unsuspecting matter and energy. She sucked the light from everything and made it a reason to party.

Now, nearly a decade later, it's clear to everyone: I'm never gonna get into the daisy dukes and I'm not going to twirl on the impromptu dance pole in the backyards. Even if I wanted to,

I'm not going to bootie pop or krump or anything that requires that much muscular coordination or energy. I'm not going to take lunch money from minors for cups of pissy kegged Coors. I'm not gonna mix screwdrivers for assholes to booze up the teen *tontas*.

My assignment seems natural to everyone except me. From now on, I'm the noz mom. Of course, Samira doesn't call it that, nor does anyone else—not to my face. Samira said, "Look girl, you've got a good watchful eye. You're a natural observer and thinker. You can assess situations. That's an asset the Ladies could really use."

What was I supposed to say to that? No one had ever found my "observation skills" to be anything but creepy or obnoxious. Worthy of nothing but a "What the fuck are you looking at?" Samira thinks it's an asset.

I watched hard for the irony to seep out of a crack in Samira's powdered face, but it remained smooth and steady, cementing with certainty what she wanted me to do.

Essentially, as noz mom, I do what I already do. I watch as the kids get sky high and then crash down from their short-lived ascent, their soft deflated bodies drooping like balloons snagged on power lines or bushes. If kids get too stupid with the gas, I go to Big Boy at the door to come check them. I'm not about to step in and intervene myself, you know.

It's the boys that I have to keep my eye on. They seem to be getting younger as the summer weeks go by. Tonight, a pack of them have checked in their trading cards and Nintendos at the door for the noz. Where are their goddam mothers? I think as I watch them suck on the balloons like it was their mama's milk filling them up again. Probably same place as my mom, I figure—sick in some bed, or biting their nails in front of the TV, or pushing fabric under an angry needle in a garment factory.

One kid's bones have turned into overcooked noodles. His friends laughed and pushed each other as they tried propping him back onto his feet, but before long, they started grunting and getting annoyed, saying, "Hey man! Enough already, your ass is heavy!" Not knowing what to do, they dropped him to the ground.

It was time to call Big Boy. Through the crowd and flashing lights, I could see that he was blocking the gate entrance with the full breadth of his body, every inch of him saying no to someone. "Big Boy!" I shouted through the noise. He chose to ignore me as he pushed back several guys, telling them "Gottapayupyougottapayup!"

"Big Boy!" I shouted like calling to a mountain, "I SAID we've got a kid down." By now, nobody likes the noz mom, squealing around every time some kids are trying to have a good time. Especially not Big Boy who has to stop them because I say so.

With a single hand, he shoved the three idiots and slammed the gate shut before charging like a bear across the patio toward the noz.

"Sit your ass down!" He grabbed the limp kid by the collar from the concrete and threw him into a plastic lawn chair. The kid slid off like cold spaghetti. Impatient, Big Boy pushed him up onto the chair again, turning around to watch the gate where one of the asshole sneaks had started to climb. The kid stayed in the chair but his head hung off the end of his spine, rolling side to side, like it was floating on gentle waves of water. "Come on dumbass, wake the fuck up!" Big Boy shook the kid hard in the chair. The kid's head flopped around helplessly. The kid was gone. "Fuck!" Big Boy saw one of the sneaks jump over the gate and disappear into the dancing crowd. He'd had it with this kid and started smacking his face, pushing it around, saying "Comeondumbasscomeondumbass!" like that was supposed to help. But it didn't, and Big Boy gave the kid a final shove on the forehead before taking off after the other guys who also jumped the gate.

The sound of a forehead splitting against concrete is one I can't bear. I kneeled on the ground, his bleeding head on my lap. I held his face in my hands and listened to him breathe. He was really a kid, maybe twelve or thirteen years old. Gone, not dreaming. Just vacant. The eyeballs under their lids had stopped rolling. So still under there I could see an emptiness so vast that I could feel myself in it.

He bled all over my hands. I called for Big Boy, who did not arrive. I held his face, all smooth and brown. He got younger, as people sometimes do in sleep. A child in my arms, he was warm and sticky. I recognized the scent of childhood through the cologne. And blood. "*Mijo, mijo*, get up. Come on, *mijo* you gotta get up." I heard my voice all trembly. "*Mijo*, please." He began to stir and nuzzled against my body. He whined softly. "*Mijo*, you better go home," I said. Suddenly he jumped and pulled his face away from me. He squinted through dark lashed slits. "Aw, fuck," he said all hoarse, as he grabbed his head with both hands. "Aw, fuck," he said again. His friends, relieved, started laughing. They elbowed each other and smacked him on the back as he pulled himself to his feet. He looked at the blood on his hands and then looked at me like I had done this to him. "Shit," he said glaring at me sideways like I was some kind of *mañosa*.

"*Pinche* noz mom," I heard him grumble.

Later, Samira gazes through the tinted windows as I tell her what happened. When I'm done, I realize she'd already heard the whole story from someone else.

"Samira, I'm pretty sure that kid's in middle school. He shouldn't have been there."

She shakes her head. "This is a new and changing world we're living in. There's no room for no goddamn babies. Boys best grow some balls cuz they are gonna need them. And ladies, we all gotta learn to use the ovaries we've got. We all gotta keep up." She shifted her eyes and fixed them, finally, on me. "You understand what I'm saying?"

And suddenly, I did. She was watching that changing world through the tinted glass and she put it right before my eyes. I recognized that darkness.

I WOKE UP to the sound of a loud truck parked in the driveway, its heavy exhaust breathing like a monster in waiting. The coded shouts and whistles of several men straightened me up. They must have been there a while because when I threw the curtains open, squinting hard through the light, they were already unloading the last tanks. Samira supervised and marked notes on her clipboard. They seemed decisive but unrushed, as if this was a thing they did routinely. As if coming to my house and unloading their shit without my permission or knowledge was something they did on a regular fucking basis.

I ran out barefoot looking around for neighbors. "Samira, it's six in the morning!" I could hardly hear my own voice over the truck engine. Samira was wrapping up the transaction, tipping the boys like some kind of Vegas kingpin.

She smiled past me, gazing into the garage. Look at her. She doesn't give a shit about me. Her hand resting so confidently on her waist. Her nails, long and arched, sharp like the blades tied to a rooster's talons.

The garage was half full with tall nitrous oxide tanks, all lined up like loyal servants of this queen. She'd taken it upon herself to clear out most of my family's personal crap, rusty tools, deflated basketballs, bags of old baby clothes. She'd had my bike fixed up. The rust and mud had all been thoroughly cleaned away, the chain was well oiled. The cracked tires and broken spokes replaced. The new chrome shone beautifully.

"Ride around on this proper bike, *mija*," is all she said without looking away from her clipboard.

I was almost too stunned for words. Illegal purchase, possession, and selling of nitrous oxide. To minors. And I'm supposed to be appeased with a bike? What am I, ten years old?

Before I could say anything I noticed that along with the obsolete heirlooms, Samira had also gotten rid of my boxes of books. They were gone. I had nothing left. Samira took all of my books.

"We've got a lot of work do, girl," Samira said looking over her notes.

I had tolerated noz, I had tolerated all of the cruelty of the Vicious Ladies and their dirty-ass parties, I had tolerated all of Samira's manipulation and tyranny, but I was not able to tolerate this.

"Samira!" I heard myself shout. "You have to stop. I won't do this. This is not right."

She looked at me with holy-like patience. Her face unrippled by my outburst.

"That's the problem with a lot of you who come back. You come here to me running around in circles trying to convince me of something. That you're right. That you've got something to bring here that we don't have, that we don't know already. And

30

the whole time I'm here watching and listening to you make all that noise doing nothing but showing me that you don't know what you're talking about. And what I gotta say is this: Shut up! Shut up and put those ideas you've got spinning around in your head to rest for a while and pay attention to how we do it here."

"Get out," I said.

THE NEXT DAY, I offered my definite resignation from the Vicious Ladies. In a solitary procession across the neighborhood, I walked my bike's newly chromed wheels over the concrete and asphalt, over burning dirt sidewalks, to the swap meet where I would find Samira. At the entrance the ticket guy usually lets me in with a nod, but this time I pushed a dollar into his window and he pushed a crumpled paper ticket back in return.

I walked the bike through the usual swap meet noise and crowd, for whom it didn't matter that it was a Tuesday, or noon, or August, or one hundred degrees. Like the Vicious Ladies, this hustle doesn't fit into the usual quadrants either. It can't. We're not gonna be in offices or factories. And so the hustle never stops.

I found Samira in her tent sitting still as a Buddha, untouchable. She sat at the center of the blue tarp tent, in the largest lawn chair I have ever seen. A throne. It was padded with cushions and draped with thick towels to absorb her slow glistening sweat.

Shining like moist clay, loose rings of skin hung from her neck and encircled her oval face. Tiny echoes in a dark pond. At the center, her laughing eyes brightened when they fell upon me. The tent flapped and billowed gently in waves, filling with the oscillating winds of the great steel fans that guarded Samira on both sides. The raucous foot traffic and noise of the swap meet was hushed, only mellow strains of bluesy oldies slipped inside. Her small son, a toddler still, crouched on a large beach towel spread on the ground that was also covered with blue tarp. He was laying out old baseball cards and crumpling them between his wet and sticky fat fingers. He looked up at me, smiling and baby-babbling.

Samira was smiling at me too. She moved as if to embrace me within the ample brown arch of her fleshy arms. Maybe she did not move at all, but merely gave the impression with even the slightest gesture of welcome. A raised Sharpie-black eyebrow. A hand uncurling fingers like the frond of a fern. I moved toward her and hugged her; she was still seated in her lawn chair. I felt her long braid against my cheek, the cool stickiness of her cleavage. Her hair smelled like almonds and vanilla and cigarettes.

"Samira," I said, "I need to be left alone. The Vicious Ladies can't come over to my house. I can't party anymore."

I could tell by her serene smile that she was unmoved. She watched me in silence, still smiling.

"Samira, you have to understand, please. I don't mean any disrespect to you or the Ladies or anyone. It's nothing personal in regards to any of you. It's personal only to me. I'm sorry, I'm sorry, I can't."

Samira seems to see right through everyone, everything. I wanted her to look at me, into me. I stood there, ready and transparent. I wanted her to look through my skin so she could see what I was feeling, that I really meant it. I wanted her to see that I loved her, that I wanted nothing more than to please her, to earn her approval, her respect, but I could not continue partying with the Ladies. I wanted her to see that I was afraid and exhausted because I couldn't tell her how afraid and exhausted I really was. She had to see it.

But I know that when I try to explain things, it instantly makes things opaque. Pulled out into the air of this world, my words merely hung between Samira and me like a cloud.

"*Mija*," Samira began, her voice filling the tent. "I'm going to tell you what it's all about but I already know you're not going to understand it. Not for a while, knowing you. It's about taking care of yourself and everyone who takes care of you. That's it. You never really got that. I know. This whole time we've had your back, we took care of you. You've been our girl because you needed us. Here, we take care of each other because no one else will. That's what the Vicious Ladies is all about. Our fathers ain't taking care of us. Our mothers ain't taking care of us. No one knows what we need like we do. All we got is each other. I'm going to take care of my girls and they're going to take care of me. That's all I know."

"Yeah but selling kids noz is not taking care of anybody."

"And you care about taking care of others?" She smiled. "Girl, you are like me. I know that you're looking for answers, something to believe in, something to save you. And I'm telling you, because I know, that there ain't no such thing. This is where you came from, this is where you grew up, this is where you came back and this is who you'll be. There's no way around it."

"What do you want?" I asked. I really wanted to know.

"The same thing you do. Why do you think I want you around? Let me ask you, what do *you* want?"

"To get out of this fucking place."

"Do you really? Why are you here now? You didn't have to come back."

"You don't understand what it's like."

"What what's like? To be smart? To look for your place in the world and not find it? Don't give me that. Girl, the truth is, you never really left. You think I didn't see you marching around the neighborhood every weekend waving around your little attitude. Or rolling on that bike like you were checking up on your very own little empire. It was cute. Kinda. In an old-school-homie way. Except it was you, a snotty skinny thing acting like she owned the place just cuz she went to college. But we were always watching. At least I was. And I wasn't sure if I wanted to kick your ass or hug the shit out of you. Let me tell you, I been around a lot longer than you. I know the neighborhood and the people who live in it like I know my own self. Even the people I don't know, I know. That's how I knew you."

Samira leaned ever so slightly from her chair, toward me.

"I like you because you're mean." Her eyes narrowed and her smile spread with tremendous pleasure.

Mean? This bully of a woman who was running a drug business from my sick mother's house was telling me that I was mean.

"Yeah. You know what I'm talking about," she said grinning with teeth I'd never seen before. "You're mean, not like some of the Ladies. You don't get up in anyone's face and talk shit. You've never even been in a fight. But in a way, you're worse than any of them."

For the first time, I knew Samira was looking at me. Really looking at me. She seemed like someone who'd just stepped out of a cutout of herself. I felt like a different person too. Something seemed to be shining all around her and reflecting onto me. As if a light had finally been turned on for the first time and we found ourselves both sitting in its glow. She did not look old at all. She was made of bronze.

"You think you're better than everyone around you. And in your own smart ways, you let them know it." Consumed in her pleasure, something both exquisite and grotesque began bubbling in her.

"You even think you're better than your own mother," she said and laughed, not the throaty cigarette laugh I expected, but clear and loud, almost girlish. Her son rolled his eyes up at us from the beach towel he was lying on, sucking on his baby bottle.

"That's okay. Our mothers don't know shit. What was the last valuable thing your mother taught you? I mean something real. Something you got from her and said, 'Hell, yeah! This is good stuff, I better hold on to this.'"

Right then and there, I saw myself more clearly than I could have ever imagined in her perfect obsidian heart. There I was, reflected back to myself in full form and great detail. It was that other me, the shadow me that I had never truly seen, except in glimpses in the corner of my eye, where they say your furtive death hides until it's the right time.

WHEN I RETURNED home, I called my mother to see how she was doing. I had not called in several weeks. My mother, who mostly slept now, my *tía* informed me, only asked for water and for me. Her illness was mysterious and had an unfamiliar name that didn't translate into anything I could look up in English, except in vague terms that referred to unresolved anger and nostalgia. Same as your grandmother, she noted. She could only be helped with the knowledge of prayers and herbs that I had never inherited or perhaps simply didn't bother to learn among all the other stuff I was hurrying to keep up with. I offered to come down to see her. My aunt fell silent before responding, "Also, you could wire money."

I hung up and remained on the mushy couch inhaling the stale air. Despite the glaring light outside, the house was dark. I took a deep breath, letting the old familiar air fill my body. Then it was time to go again.

EAT THE MOUTH THAT
FEEDS YOU

~~~~~

MY DAUGHTER, FOR lack of memory, eats me. Sometimes in little bites throughout the day. I don't even notice it until I feel a dull pain in the ribs and see it is my daughter, chewing on the meat around the small bone. She sucks blood from the veins while she reads one of her books on the couch. When I hear her crunching on the bone to suck the marrow, I pretend not to notice, and I remember to rush back to the kitchen to check on a pot I left on the fire. I am here to feed her, what can I do.

Sometimes my daughter, she is cruel, sometimes she bites into my flesh but not enough to cut far into the skin. And she watches me in her grip. Sometimes I start to pull away, sometimes I cry out and my eyes fill with tears. Sometimes without thinking I will say, "Why do you hurt me? You are so cruel." But it's not fair for me to say those things. It is her right. She must take those things. She must take from me what she needs.

It's because I don't have answers to her questions. I don't know what to say, I never have the words or I don't understand her questions. She asks me things I don't know how to answer. She accuses me of things that don't make sense.

She started by eating the letters my mother sent me every month. When she was very young, I'd read them to her with the usual news: "Your sister Adriana is unbearable with her flirting all over the place with the older men. Your brother Octavio is very good at math but fights too much. And your father...well, you know. Remember, if the baby is crying too much, check if her teeth are coming. Give her an onion to chew on."

My daughter loved to smell the letters and touch the thin, lined paper with her fat palms. Sometimes they smelled of chewing gum, a flat stick folded between the ruled sheets for my daughter. She would lick the paper, still smelling of spearmint, lick the papers with her little tongue and smear the ink. She'd put creased pages into her mouth and let them soak and she'd suck and she'd suck until the ink bled through and stained her tongue. "What are you doing?" I said. Her mouth, it looked like blood but it was ink, the corners of her mouth dripping black saliva. "Drink this," I said. "Drink this milk. Drink it."

Even as she got older, she liked the feel of the paper, soft, almost creamy when moistened with saliva, sliding down the throat. I wondered if it could get stuck there, or if she'd papier-mâché her insides eating all that paper. Would it form a delicate cast of all her organs, would the walls make a maze? Or would it spell out beautiful poems or complicated songs, the kind you never want to end? Now I imagine it might look like the inside of a house. I know my daughter's house will be beautiful one day. Over the years, she has eaten enough pencils and erasers, nibbled on wooden rulers, sipped on ink from the tips of pens, and has chewed on enough paper to create a beautiful blueprint. Her insides will be a beautiful house and she'll play music I won't understand but it'll be like when you play the B side of an album you bought because you heard the popular songs on the radio. I have learned to love those B-side songs best of all. If you listen enough times, you will too.

But my daughter, she also ate fistfuls of dirt. Into her mouth went black wet earth, dirt crumbs, some veiny leaves, and dried mud. She ate sand at the park, ground her teeth on the hard grains until they became fine dust. Once we were visiting my family and my daughter, she was with my sister, the single one. They sat on the lumpy bed looking at old love letters and cards and stuffed animals. They were sitting on the bed. They were eating something. It was clay. They were breaking off shards of a small pot and eating it like very fine chocolate. My sister she said to me, It still tastes like the river, you can remember the river like this, you can remember the waters, sweet like milk, do you remember, sister? You can remember us when we were kids and you'd help carry the little ones on your hip all the way, taste it you'll remember. I took a piece, it was a dark clay, smooth and cool when you put it on your tongue but grainy and crumbly between your teeth. My daughter chewed and chewed, watching me. I tasted the earth and I tasted the river. It was true. I could remember the little ones shivering wet in the river with their droopy underwear soggy in the sun. I said yes, I remember. I could see our family in the shade of a large tree, spread out on a large blanket. Me in my sundress, cradling the baby. I always thought it was a little funny and embarrassing the way they snuggled against my new breasts. Hey baby, I'm your sister, not your mom! My face was round then like the moon and there was so much more of me, hips already wide beneath the full skirts, waist cinched tight.

Now look at me, *mija*. Take whatever you can now. There's not much. I don't know how much more I have to give.

I let her eat me. And I will go in there even though I'm afraid, but she's already eaten my mother and my grandmother. But she didn't eat them like she eats me. They're already dead. She ate their letters, all of them, even though I hid them from her knowing she'd look for them. Then she ate their photographs. The photograph of my mother before she married my father. My father, despite his good looks, his greased-up hair and creased pants, pales next to her mouth, though pretty, already curling into a sneer. I saw my daughter swallow the photograph, her own lips learning to sharpen into that scythe. When she ate my grandmother's photograph, my daughter looked at me bewildered. It was that photograph of my grandmother when she was already a mother, had already given birth to all of her children. But she sat on a beach, wearing a bathing suit, and shared a tall can of beer with another woman. Where was my mother? Where were her siblings? My grandfather? There was no trace of my mother, nor of me. In our faces, theirs and mine, there were no shared traces. Since always, our paths had been broken. And yet we insisted on finding our way back to each other.

The last time we visited my mother's home, the home where I was raised, the summer after my mother died, I thought my daughter went too far. She went into their bedrooms, which no one wanted to touch or change because we still believed my mother or grandmother might walk right back in, my mother huffing and puffing from the market heavy with vegetables, coffee, bits of tripe. Or my grandmother shuffling her slippers back into the house after sweeping the dirt and bad spirits off their sidewalk, onto the street. All of us, the brothers and sisters, we wanted our mother and grandmother to remember their way back into the house and find all of their things right where they left them. But my daughter, who does not remember things the way we do, who hardly has any memory at all, she came into the rooms and started pulling open the drawers, flipping through notebooks, opening the doors of the old wardrobes and smelling their contents, running and pushing her hands through everything, licking and gnawing on edges and corners. She wasn't even really looking at anything. Then she opened the jars of beauty creams and licked the lids and yellowing rims, and then she scooped out cold cream with her fingers and ate it. She ate all of it. Then she went through the perfume bottles and sipped the amber elixirs, she gulped down bottles of holy waters my mother had carried from blessed wells, she sucked the sugar skeletons my grandmother brought from Guanajuato, chewed on wax prayer candles and plastic rosary beads. The family, they always thought my daughter was a little crazy. Now they think she is possessed.

But now I'm beginning to understand. Now I know what she is doing. For now, the best I can do is let her eat whatever she needs and wants. I am relieved that I know now where to find my mother and grandmother. They are inside my daughter.

There's nothing I want more than to be with them again. We will live in the house my daughter has built and I'll listen to all of the records and learn the words and maybe even dance again like I used to when I was a very young woman, and my hair will be long and loose again swinging in the room filled with music, the record player playing and playing. But this time it'll be different because when my brother comes looking for me, since my mother sends him every time, I will keep dancing. And when she comes looking for me herself and when she looks at me in that way, I will be very hungry and I will be ready. I'll grab a bite from her and chew on her plump flesh, her skin so smooth and soft in my mouth.

I'll start by taking a bite out of her forearm, which is the body part I remember the most. It will be soft and dark and taste like the armrest of her chair and it will taste like the shade of the house, it will taste like clean tile and wet cement. My mother, she will pull away from me, think that I'm possessed by the devil while I swallow her. It was just a little bite. She won't be able to speak not knowing what to do with her arm, usually for keeping everyone at bay. And maybe, once I start eating I won't be able to stop. I'll eat her all up.

Then I'll understand all of it. I'll understand my mother. I'll understand my daughter. I'll say, Ah, so this is it. I will say, I understand you now my daughter because with the taste of my mother in my mouth, with her flesh in my body and her blood in my veins I will understand her, too. My mother, I don't know, but I believe she will also understand once she's inside of me, the way I'm beginning to understand now inside of my daughter. Then she will see what she has to do.

MYSTERIOUS BODIES

~~~~~

ANGELICA FELT HEAVY and petrified, as the walls of her belly slowly began to bubble and blister. She breathed deeply to contain the seething, crackling little boils. But this time their angry hunger could not be appeased and they continued to spread and mount, bursting into voracious mollusks, clams and barnacles that gnawed incessantly at her throbbing meat. They attached themselves to the walls of her stomach and reproduced quickly, spreading out over her intestines and up into her lungs, they began to chew into her ribs, crawl up her esophagus. She was dripping inside with salty saliva from their muscled tongues that were also teeth. She could hear them furiously scraping against each other, blindly tearing into her organs, swallowing her bit by bit into their encrusted shells, anxious to exhaust her mottled innards until there was nothing left but a dry hull.

Reduced to a fragile, extinguished shell, Angelica's emptied body stood silently out in the open against the wind, pierced by the sun, until finally she flaked into dry shards and collapsed into the sand. Surrendering to the peace, she completely lost consciousness.

Eduard saw a transformation take place, but from his perspective, one minute Angelica listened to him go over the his day's business agenda, and the next minute she dissolved from her seat onto the restaurant floor like a paper napkin in the wind. Her *torta de jamón* and *papas a la francesa* remained untouched in the plastic basket on the table.

When Angelica finally pushed open her heavy eyelids, through a hazy light she recognized Eduard's face, his eyes, nose, lips hovering over her. But the expression he bore on his familiar features she could not quite place, and she suddenly wondered where she was. Instead of the crackle of hungry mollusks and hissing tide, she began to discern other whispering voices. She realized that instead of a solitary beach she was laid out on the hard tile of a crowded TortasPlus, and she quickly pulled on Eduard's sleeves and grappled with his arms and hands to get onto her feet and out the door.

"Angelica, are you listening to me?"

The blaring daylight and roaring street induced a sense of deep calm.

"Angelica, I don't want you to take any more pills."

The light had changed. The air had cleared. She was aware of the sound of her footsteps on the asphalt. All around her, the city vibrated.

"Did you hear me?"

She felt synchronized, part of a familiar rhythm, assured that she knew exactly what to do.

"Angelica, sit down, I'm serious."

Eduard sat her down onto a park bench in a large open plaza. A parade of young cadets rigidly saluted the flag as they passed by.

He had that look on his face again. She remembered it now. It was that troubled look he had six months ago when his snakes got sick. "Angelica," she remembered him saying softly, almost in tears, "they're dying, they won't eat, they're as limp as noodles, all of them." What was he going to do? He was supposed to deliver their venom to the lab days ago. They had been calling, reminding him, demanding, threatening to go with another venom vendor. They'd tell the other labs about him, ruin his hard-earned reputation.

He was screwed without his snakes. And what's more, he really loved them.

Angelica always wanted him to look at her that way, with that much attention and intensity that would show he loved her that much too. That he needed her around. And finally here it was.

"No more pills, Angelica. You're going to end up killing yourself."

She saw that his concern was real, as was the conviction of his decision.

"No more pills. Do you hear me?" he said, looking at her intently, holding her face in his hands.

"Yes, I heard you." She watched the worry instantly melt from his face. That's all Eduard needed to hear. He gave her an energetic kiss on her closed lips.

"We'll find another way, you'll see," he said, already fixing his sights on the interrupted day's agenda.

Ordinarily, she would have conceded to his decision. The display of genuine concern and affection that she had been craving would have instantly snuffed out any doubts. But somehow it didn't matter anymore. What mattered now was the clarity and the stillness that she now firmly possessed.

Angelica did not know the original use of the white pills Eduard purchased when they had already taken every suggestion, superstition and story as a sign of hope that would rescue them from the future threatening to swallow them both alive. She had already taken an infinite variety of bitter herbs and teas that helped preserve the dignities of young ladies gone astray. Eduard took her to a *curandera*, who promised to solve their dilemma with chants, smoking leaves, and oily rubdowns. In desperation, they began to fill her petite body with a stream of pharmaceutical chemicals.

Eduard bartered for the pills from a business friend, Alex, who quietly slipped them out of the pharmacy where he worked in exchange for several hundred pesos and a newborn iguana. He was an expert in the alternate uses of prescription medicine, and dedicated himself to discovering qualities that most chemists or pharmacists didn't know about, but which today's youth sought out and deeply appreciated. Some pills successfully endowed the purchasing youth with the superhuman energy necessary to meet the rigorous demands of urban recreation and survival. Among his most consistent clientele were the Italian rastafarians. In their crusade to spread the religion of electronic music throughout Latin America, these self-proclaimed rave missionaries sought Alex's aid to keep the pulsing, throbbing, flailing of so many young bodies dancing through the night. Alex prescribed a method to make this possible. In addition, guided by his own sensitivities, Alex took it upon himself to formulate pharmaceutical nuances that allowed young ravers to ride smoothly into the Sunday morning dawn and delivered them on time to their seats before their grandmothers' steaming *menudo*.

The pills were also useful for enduring long chases through the city, running through back alleys and flying over walls and fences to escape the claws and bullets of the police. But of course, every once in a while, the little pill failed some ill-fated young man who plummeted to the ground like a shot pigeon, splattering the concrete with drops of deep red blood, ephemeral rubies that transformed into brown stains, lost among ancient gum, drunkards' dried vomit, and spilled Coca-Cola.

Alex eventually realized that survival depended not only on a state of heightened physical capacity—it must be complemented by a steady mental state, a peace of mind that hardly comes naturally nowadays. The second most popular pills were useful for grasping at least a few moments of complete tranquility—an enrapturing nebulous nirvana, infinite and untouchable peace.

In addition, through his rigorous experimentations, Alex had stumbled upon another unforeseen yet very useful quality of a particular sack of these nirvana-inducing pills. Although they only seemed to be good for treating symptoms of inflamed spleen, they were also useful in discharging undesired fetuses from the bodies of terrified young girls who searched desperately for some way to rip out the dark, uncertain futures that grew in their mysterious wombs.

Alex had prescribed these little white pills to Laura, a high school friend. She asked him for something to help her arrive at a state of complete bliss. She wanted nothing else than to feel as profoundly content as she had one time, the previous winter while running among the pines of Manantlán, when she was caught off guard by the pink of dawn as it peeked through the treetops. It was as if she were about to enter the rose-colored interior of a great conch shell illuminated by the sun.

When she swallowed the pills and waited for its effects for several long hours, she felt disappointed. Fuckin' Alex, he ripped me off, she thought. But after a while, she felt death ripping her womb to shreds. Sweating thick drops of agony, she dragged herself across her bedroom floor. It took several hours and finally, exhausted, she reached the cool bathroom tile and managed to lift herself slowly onto the toilet. Just as she sat, she felt something drop suddenly from the depths of her body, from a center so profound that it was a mystery even to her. It was the point where the body unites with the soul and intersects, like that unreachable point on the horizon where the ocean meets the sky. And she felt intensely relieved. After so much, so much pain, it was like finally finding a peace she had not felt since that day in the woods.

Laura had had no idea that while she thought she was alone, inside her body a tiny seed had gestated and taken root, a palpitation of cells that was replicating ceaselessly, taking on a shape for the world outside.

Angelica, on the other hand, could not escape the nightmare that accompanied her day and night, awake and asleep, everywhere she went. It was something that grew more monstrous and terrifying with every passing instant.

Her period had not come. And it would not, no matter how she and Eduard tried to draw it out. That's when she began to feel the tiny hard bubbles, membranes hardening into a cluster of live shells that bit and buried themselves into her womb. They were hungry, siphoning her from the inside out. And no one could help her. Without knowing it at first, the answer began to crystallize inside of her.

Meanwhile, Eduard spent long nights sweating and tossing in his bed. He stared at the stucco ceiling like watching a great mystical screen where his tragic destiny was projected. He saw Angelica's father, a terrible, giant ranchero with blond hair, spewing furious foam at the mouth as he approached him with merciless brutality. The sky was covered by the fine beige fabric of his vaquero suit, which was impeccably complemented by his cowboy hat. His boots were made of a grotesque patchwork of crocodile and ostrich skin, identical to his thick belt that displayed an enormous buckle the size of a license plate. In elegant calligraphy, his initials, H.R.S., were engraved. Eduard knew that for other reasons, these initials were among the most feared in the state of Jalisco. H.R.S. spelled exploding kaleidoscopes of shattered car windshields, American guns, clutters of blessed candles, photos, and flowers.

And finally, on that mystical screen Eduard saw two monstrous gold chains descending over his head. First he saw a breathtaking medallion of the Virgencita de Guadalupe, with her lovely little merciful face delicately engraved in the shining metal. And just as he began to feel a sense of comfort and relief, a tremendous crucifix interrupted his peace, with razor thorns finely carved into the agonized face of Christ.

ALONE IN HER bedroom, Angelica swallowed the remaining contents of the plastic baggie, thrice the amount Alex had instructed. She remembered herself from just days ago, trembling as if she were about to collapse as he put the sack of small chalky pills in her hand. She looked to Eduard to steady her. He seemed as confident as if it were any other business transaction while he pulled the baby iguana out his backpack, swaddled in a soft pink washcloth. He petted the sleepy reptile affectionately with his finger, nudged its tiny snout with his lip before handing it over to Alex with the money.

"Take good care of my baby," he said. Alex laughed.

Angelica saw herself standing there in silence, clutching the baggie in her sweaty palm. She couldn't recognize that girl anymore, quivering, not solid, not liquid, made of another substance, unstable particles, vulnerable to air, a coagulated thing on the verge of melting or toppling over.

Now, standing alone with the emptied baggie, she held onto something else that kept her firm, unwavering, unhesitant. She felt her body dampen and she focused on the mollusks again. She opened herself to their voracious habitation, their decisive devouring. They ate through her skin and began to eat each other until they formed a single, continuous, thick shell, replacing the body that had once been hers. Calcified and strengthened, she was ready for the transformation that was to come.

She sat on the ivory toilet seat, gripping the ceramic bowl. She was bright, clear, crystallized. Inside of her, a boiling mass of flesh, the thousands of agitated, muscled tongues growled, trying to form a language of their own. The twisting and knotting and tearing in her womb grew into a churning vortex, filling her belly, gaining force, sucking into its hungry, gaping mouth all of the shapeless pulp that filled her body. Sucking the walls of her ribs into the vacuum of its center, pulling in muscles, ligaments, nerves, veins, organs, liquefying bone. She ground her teeth to offer as well. Her skull cracked, her cranium was splitting, pulled into a knowing void, a relentless hole, an unquestionable core, a wonderful exhalation.

CRYSTAL PALACE

~~~~~~

LOOK *MIJA,* WHEN I was maybe seventeen or eighteen years old, I worked at a boutique selling fancy French beauty products, over there in Guadalajara.

The boutique was luxurious, with crystals and mirrors everywhere. Everything sparkled like a diamond, even the little glass bottles filled with the fine lotions. But I felt a bit nervous there, you know, like if I moved too quickly or carelessly I would break something. I was used to doing things using my strength and with *ganas.* That's how my amá taught me. You do things with *ganas,* *mija,* she would say to me. With *ganas* you pick up the kids, my little brothers, to wipe off the dirty snot dripping from their noses. With *ganas* you scrub your father's hard denim pants over the *lavadero* and with *ganas* you sweep our part of the street so that no one can say we are not clean people.

But in this place, La Freu Freu, it was called, you did everything very delicately. "With finesse, my dear," the Señora Sanz, my boss, would say. "Look," she would correct me, lifting her tiny little nose. Then she would demonstrate how my work was to be done. With the tippy tips of her fingers she would pick up a tiny flask containing some precious fluid and carefully place it on the glass display case. You could hear the sweet little sound, a *ting*, like a little bell, every time she showed me how it should be done.

I had the habit of taking the glass bottles and jars five at a time, picking them up and securing them against my breasts, soft and safe. You better believe that breasts are the safest place to keep important things. This is where I keep my coin purse, and mind you, I have never had a single cent stolen. Of course, it's safe so long as you keep it that way and you don't allow busy hands to make their way in there. But to each her own *chi chis*, I always say.

This is how I would set up the boutique more quickly, pressing the precious containers against my breasts, until one day la Señora Sanz came in with her little shoes going *clic clic clic* over the polished floor, and she screamed so suddenly that it made me jump with fright.

"*¡Dios mío!*" she shrieked.

I dropped all of the glass jars and bottles, and they broke into a million pieces on the checkered tiles. The floor was splattered with precious white creams, like the pigeon shit that covered the plaza outside

"Such a stupid girl!" she screamed at me, spitting out the words between her pearly teeth and red lips. "What are you doing? You are a careless fool, a brute!"

It was the first time anyone who was not my mother had screamed at me that way. I stood there stunned with my hands hanging at my sides and my breath frozen in my lungs.

"How could you carry these things in that way? *¿Cómo se te ocurre?* These," she said pointing at the white puddle on the floor with her sharp fingernail, "these are fine products."

Still frozen, watching her red mouth and pearly teeth open and close, close and open, I thought, "What does she mean, *¿cómo se me ocurre?*" This was the only way I knew how to do things carefully and well. Just that way, in the safety of my hands and breasts I carried the finest, most delicate things in the whole world. This was how I carried my little brothers and sisters from one place to another, *de aquí pa'allá.* Just imagine what would happen to me if I ever dropped one of them and broke their head. What did she mean, how I could carry these things that way? I couldn't understand what this woman standing in front of me, moving her jaws, waving her arms and bony hands, was saying.

"A hopeless brute!" continued the Señora Sanz. When she saw my confusion, she moved to show me what she meant.

She gathered her rage, rearranging loosened strands of hair back into her hairdo. She licked the specks of saliva off her lips and walked with her little high heels *clic clic clic* to the display case. She took a tiny jar from a box and fixed her eyes on mine while she explained, "Look dear, in this boutique, we only have the best of the best. Here, only the best of the best people come in through our doors. This is not a place for stupidities, or clumsiness. We save those for the flea market."

Although the bits of glass that shattered across the floor hadn't touched me, I felt wounded anyway. I stood there remembering the Ponds cold creams and Avon perfumes that my mother and I bought from Doña Cosme on Thursdays at the market, I felt something deep inside me hurt, as if a splinter of glass had somehow penetrated my heart.

"I am going to have to ask you to please be more careful. And this must never happen again. Now, get to work and clean up this mess." She placed the tiny crystal bottle onto the illuminated display case and walked off, leaving me standing there alone at the counter.

I stood without moving for several minutes, staring at that stupid little thing, so delicate, so pretty. To me, it seemed as precious as a jewel. It was something my hands were never meant to touch. And suddenly, I felt terrified, afraid to move, since any clumsy gesture of mine could make the entire crystal palace come tumbling down, and those marvelous elixirs of eternal beauty and infinite perfection would be lost forever.

I could feel my bones growing thick, my legs and arms like monstrous tree trunks. My breasts transformed into tremendous masses of flesh, mountains, dormant volcanoes. My feet seemed enormous and permanently disfigured from going around barefoot most of my life. My face was far too wide to turn and look at my surroundings, so brilliant, cold, and sharp.

I stood there motionless for a long time, afraid to even breathe lest I stir up a cyclone. I waited, taking tiny sips of air until I shrank back down to a size that would not cause a disaster. I stepped forward warily, measuring each one of my movements. Slowly I mopped the floor and carefully cleaned every surface. When I had finished, I bent over to pick up my *morral* from behind the register, making sure my butt had enough space so as not to destroy yet another magical potion. All I wanted was to leave. I crossed the boutique as silently and quickly as possible and, turning off the lights behind me, I locked up and hurried out into the evening wind.

I walked and walked, staring at the broken pavement and black gum spots, eager to leave that place far behind. After a few blocks, I began to feel more at peace, making my way through the black streets illuminated with crude lights and neon signs blinking all around, with the bars, the bakeries, the bookstores. When I got to the bus stop, I stood beneath a naked light bulb at a *churro* booth and, finally exhaling out all the breath I'd been holding, I asked for a two-peso *churro*, please.

What a day, *Dios Santo*. What a *pinche día*. Who would have thought it would be so traumatic to work at a beauty boutique? Although my body had returned to its regular size, I was still hurting inside and preferred not to think about what had happened. I just wanted to get home so I could take off my pantyhose, the tight shoes, and slip my feet into my favorite pair of tire-soled huaraches, so broken-in and soft. I wanted to put on my apron to help my *amá* make supper for the kids. I wanted to be standing in the kitchen, in front of the tin *comal* with hot tortillas in my hands, warming the milk for the little ones to drink from their clay cups. I wanted to kiss my *amá* on the cheek and hold baby Tavo in my arms.

I suddenly remembered that in my fright and embarrassment, I'd forgotten my pay at work. Imagine that, *mija! Híjole*, what a dummy! I had to go back for it now, because tomorrow *amá* and I had to pay Don Fermín for the beans he let us take on credit. And there was nothing my mother hated more than owing people money.

I didn't want to go back to La Freu Freu, but I didn't have a choice. I thought, well at least that Doña wouldn't be there and I still had the key to open up. I'd just get my little envelope with my little money and in a flash I'd be on my way home again.

When I arrived at the boutique, everything was dark. All you could see were black silhouettes. That luminous salon of crystals and mirrors and sparkling surfaces was transformed into an opaque space, a puzzle of shadows and weak echoes of streetlights.

As I approached the glass door, I heard a voice coming from inside.

"Arturo, honey. It's just that I don't understand..." It was the voice of la Señora Sanz.

"Arturo, please. I beg you." I froze and held my breath. It was the voice of la Señora, but at the same time, it wasn't. It was somehow different. I had never heard her like that.

"Arturo, please, don't do this to me. For the love of god..."

It wasn't the hard, sharp voice that I knew. This voice was soft, full of pain, and fear too, I think. I heard when she started to cry, and I just didn't know what to do. She cried with sighs that shook out from the depths of her chest. I was afraid to move but I dared to shift my eyes to look inside, and when they adjusted to the kaleidoscope of shadows I could see her leaning against the counter with the telephone to her ear.

Her meticulous hairdo had tumbled into a fragile chaos over her face. She tried to silence her sobs by biting her lips. The red of her lipstick had crossed her cheek.

"Arturo, no more. I can't take this any more," she implored. "Please..."

Was this really la Señora Sanz? I couldn't believe it. This woman clawing at her hair, her face and chest with so much desperation, was this la Señora Sanz?

"Arturo," she continued. "Arturo, no more. No more. NO MORE! Son of a bitch, no more!!!"

And right then la Señora went crazy and threw the telephone against a mirror. She swiped her bony arm across the length of the display case and sent bottles and jars flying.

"You son of a bitch!!!" she screamed, throwing whatever was within her reach until she had flung the very last jar of Ultra-Softening Anti-Cellulite cream, shattering it to pieces. She let herself fall to the floor with great sobs that shook her entire body. Her hair covered her face as she cradled herself in her own arms. She just cried and cried lying there. I don't know how long she cried. I decided to leave, without a sound, and go home. I would pick up my pay the next day. Don Fermín could wait a little longer for his money.

I turned away, walking back to the bus stop. I could hear her sobs for a long time as they continued to echo in my mind. I listened until they finally dissolved, joining the lament of a police siren on its slow, persistent way through the emptying streets. And then came the voice of Lola Beltrán, one of her weeping songs floating from the window of a passing car, calling down the summer rain from the darkness of the sky.

TORTILLAS BURNING

~~~~~

WHEN YOU'VE GOT nothing else, you'll always have at least a tortilla to get you through. Learn to use them. Take a tortilla, an old one that's gone hard, and hold it over a flame. Watch the tortilla blacken and break. Take those ashes, when you have nothing else, take the ashes and rub them onto your teeth with your fingers. Smudge them, scrub them over your gums, all over inside your mouth. *Con un buche de agua,* rinse and spit into the ground. Rinse very well, lest anyone confuse you with a witch. *La gente es bien pendeja.* Like they don't know the brujas are often the most beautiful. Careful with the *bonitas,* I say. One minute they are the sweetest pair of honeyed calves dripping down the street, and the next they're owl wings beating the night air. But not us. Not too pretty, though we have our gifts, we keep our teeth clean, our floors swept.

The things my grandmother used to say.

I often wondered what kind of situation would require me to burn a tortilla to clean my teeth. When might I be without basic items like toothpaste or bath soap, so that I'd have to find some elemental alternative to perform simple personal hygiene? It was hard to imagine what kind of thing might happen that would knock you back to where your grandmother had been.

It's a wonder even to me how I ended up on that pig farm. I wasn't meant for farm life, you know. Good at math, I was still going to high school and everything, kept my socks up but my skirt short like all the other girls, playing hooky on the Malecón whenever we were sure we'd get away with it. My own mother, *qué en paz descanse* was no saint, just normal like me. But when you're a girl of seventeen, and a man, young and handsome, looks you in the eye, serious, unlike the clowns you grew up with, and he tells you to marry him, well you think, why not? Here was a man, like a door, instead of a hole or a rope. Formal and upright. But I didn't think to ask where I'd end up with him on the other side of that door. He was opaque that way, didn't give many clues, but I should have known better with all that dust that covered him. That dust. That's where I went—a place full of dust. Americans think Mexico is green and lush, a big resort hotel and a pyramid in a jungle by the sea. Well why wouldn't they? They just jump on their American Airline and off they go, skipping over everything, the dust and the rocks, the farms and the factories, and even the cities. They arrive at Cancún or Puerto Vallarta with their shoes clean and they find an ocean fit for a white bikini.

Or that's what I've heard. I haven't returned since.

The dust is what I most remember about living on the farm. Dust everywhere, always. One spends the day trying to keep the tile clean, when it might just as well have been made of dirt. You can imagine. Sweeping and sweeping, dusting and dusting and nothing ever gets clean. *Polvo eres y en polvo te convertirás.* Every day was Ash Wednesday, somber with ashy doom marked upon you no matter how bright the sun. It was this life, pressed upon my forehead every year of my childhood, a reminder from

God, his sinister plan always there waiting for me, and I'd finally arrived to it. As a girl, laughing and sneaking drinks with the boys, it was hard to believe the Sunday litanies or the abuelitas' threats, but then one day you're Alicia following a white rabbit down the hole or a through a door. It was always there, waiting for you. *Bienvenida.* This is your *país* now. These are your *maravillas.*

My Luisito really was a *maravillla,* I could hardly believe it. A perfect baby, a perfect boy. Now on his way to being a man, and believe me, I've taught him not to be any kind of rabbit. Along with the dusty floors and shelves and pots and pans and everything else, I constantly wiped him clean, as if to clear him of any fate that was bound to that place. I did my best to keep his nose and his knees clean, but you know how kids are, especially boys. In my heart I prayed, over and over I'd whisper to him like a little song, not here, not this place, not like your father, not this life. *Más allá, más allá, el mundo es grande como tu corazón. Es un círculo, un cír-cu-loooo, no tiene fin. Ven, con tu dedito, trace a circle, te amo te amo te amo sin fin.* Lord knows, I've always tried my best.

Martín, his father, now a name like flakes of rust on my tongue, would come home smelling like pig shit and beer, but it was his bad mood that bothered me the most. He always came home looking for reasons to yell, mostly at me. Nothing I did pleased him. As if it were my fault that we lived on a pig farm or as if it were my fault that we never had enough money or as if it were my fault that I got pregnant with Luis too soon and spoiled whatever fairy tale plans he had for our life. I was only seventeen.

One day, normal like any other day, he came home for dinner. He took his seat at the table without a word, which was not unusual because I'd learned he was not a man of many words except when he was angry. Both hands waiting on the table for his food, I could feel him searching in his silence. Luis had just turned three years old and ran around the house like an unleashed puppy, so thrilled was he to see his *papá*. We hardly saw anyone at the time. I was standing over the *comal*, flipping the tortillas when I heard a crash followed by the hard scrape of Martín's chair over the gritty tile. As I ran from the kitchen I could hear him spitting out his *malhabladas*, barking like a rabid dog. By the time I got to them, he was already taking off his belt to whip my little boy. Luis had knocked down a small, framed portrait of Martín's parents. The photograph and the frame seemed fine, but the glass was shattered. It was just glass.

That belt was probably the most expensive thing in the house. When he bought it, we hardly had a thing to eat for a week. There I was, asking for *tortillas y frijoles* on credit, a strip of meat for the baby, scrounging around the garden for *acelgas* or *quelites*, whatever weeds I knew wouldn't poison us because the pigs ate them. I never would have imagined it in my youth, my recent childhood when it was not hard to have a coin for a treat. Not a thing of this did I mention to my mother in my letters, but when we talked on the phone once a month I'm sure she could hear something was wrong. I could hear something hollow in my own words when I repeated that everything was fine. To console me in my secret hardship, but probably to console herself, my mother said it was always hard in the early years of a family. But a family learns to grow together through its hardships. Perhaps she was right, but from what I could remember, I'd not been born into this kind of poverty. I didn't have the space for hunger built into my body. But now, I learned to build it for myself so that the baby would not suffer it. There's a way to make room for hunger, to hold it, embrace it. But this was a lonely hunger, the kind that separates you from others, and that's what hurts the most. I hope you will never have to learn this.

I was bewildered by the exquisite belt, more valuable than my life. I understood this when he first brought it home, laid it on the bed coiled like a baby serpent. I'd seen *cintos piteados* before on our trips to town, but none this ornate. An elaborate design patterned its length, bunches of roses and vines bursting with morning glories, one antlered deer kissed stalks of grass, another kissed the sky. Stitched in fine maguey threads, a landscape of hills was fashioned in the background of glyphs. Its geometries spoke an ancient language we'd learned in our blood to decipher. Its beauty clued me in to the misery that would follow.

And when I saw that this *viejo desgraciado* was about to turn his belt on my son, I threw myself to protect him with my own body. The leather was thick but I toughened myself against it as it landed on my ribs. I pulled the baby aside, I can still hear him screaming, and I stood up to this man, pushed myself right up to his face to let him know I was not afraid. He would not make less of me. I was never meek, but Martín had never seen me like this, and I could see the surprise light up his expression, before it turned into a fire. That's when he punched me in the face, knocked me right to the ground. But even then I would not yield to him, already pushing myself up on all fours when he whipped me on the back. I bit my lips so as to not scream, I saw my boy's eyes fixed on me. I crawled to him and curled myself around his shivering little body, to muffle his cries with my bosom. That beast crunched his face into a scowl, locked his lips like he'd had the last word.

As soon as he slammed the front door shut behind him, I grabbed the baby and ran for my things, my purse and a handful of clothes and that was it. You'd be surprised by how little you need when you're running for your life. The last thing I remember was seeing Martín's food still on the table and thinking about the tortillas I'd left on the *comal* smoking over the gas flame. I let them burn.

SÁBADO GIGANTE

~~~~~~

EMMANUEL FEELS THE drops of sweat gathering on his scalp. He picks his fingers through his curls, careful not to break the shiny shellac of gel and hairspray that keeps his hair from fluffing up into a freakish mess. He wipes the warm moisture off his upper lip and crosses his arms again across his chest.

From his seat backstage, he watches the spectacle on a monitor and jumps at the shrill verdict of the trumpet as it pierces the studio and stabs right into his ear. Emmanuel drops his head and wipes his lip again. It is almost his turn.

The woman on stage gets another try and the band starts up again with her song. Shaken by her first failed attempt, she forces herself back into the salsa rhythm, frowning to find the brassy beat. But her red lips, trained to smile despite circumstance, her middle-aged body wrapped in a shimmering sequined dress, and her ankles being visibly choked by the straps of her shoes, all of her refuses defeat. Don Francisco dances around her, balancing his towering red-and-white-striped Dr. Seuss hat with one hand and holding the microphone with the other.

El Chacal stands stiffly at attention to the side, with his trumpet already poised at the gold-sequined aperture of his mouth.

In his velvety black hood, he is a glam executioner ready to kill dreams and maim dignity.

Though this is a song she clearly loves and knows well, the woman opens her mouth and releases a long nasal squawk. El Chacal promptly blows his trumpet at the first ghastly note.

The audience howls with laughter and with Don Francisco taking the lead, they roar "*¡Fuera! ¡Fuera! ¡Fuera!*" swinging their arms and fingers in a wave toward the back door. This is not a sympathetic crowd. But Emmanuel didn't come here for sympathy. He learned to get by without it long ago.

As if a choreographed rejection wasn't enough, a man in a lion costume charges onstage and pounces on the woman. The spectacle becomes too much even for her as she covers her face with her hands, and the lion drags her across the stage, disappearing through a curtain of gold streamers, the points of her high heels trailing like punctuation. Emmanuel exhales.

Next contestant. Emmanuel can hardly bear it. But he must to do this. There are no other options. It's been too long already. This is his time.

He knows that people in every corner in Latin America are watching. *Sábado Gigante* is *Jerry Springer*, *Miss Latin America*, *National Geographic*, *Comedy Central*, *The Price Is Right*, *Star Search* and a burlesque show all at once, strung together by catchy jingles for Colgate, Kraft and McDonalds, which the entire audience sings and dances together during three hours of gospel-like reverie. *Sábado Gigante* really is *gigante*.

There is no doubt in Emmanuel's mind that his father will be watching. Emmanuel knows he'll be astounded to see how his son, his namesake, has grown into such a strong, talented man, despite 29 years of utter neglect. Sharp pangs of regret would surely pierce his heart.

Emmanuel knows he has to go through with this. He knows that these days, no Spanish-singing artist can ever amount to anything more than a *quinceañera* party entertainer, unless the Estefans pull you under their wing. And now here he is in Miami, far far from home, waiting deep in the gut of the Univisión Studios for the moment to bring his talent to the world spotlight.

Emmanuel has always hated El Chacal de la Trompeta. El Chacal humiliates people with no talent and mostly sends home the not-so-bad ones along with the pretty-good with a blast of his brain-ripping horn. Often the winner was a mediocre singer who was typically shy, young and pretty, and who let Don Francisco squeeze them and "accidentally" kiss them on the lips. But every once in a while an indisputably great singer would wow everyone and take the prize. Today would be that kind of day, he is certain.

Just a few more minutes now. Don Francisco introduces the next contestant. Her name is Karina Ochoa, resident of *Nueva Yersey*, she's a college student and a teacher's aide and here to sing Whitney Houston's interpretation of "I Will Always Love You."

A lean, very young woman with long hair walks across the stage with a microphone. She pulls her hair back behind her ear, smiling sheepishly. Don Francisco emerges with a huge yellow cowboy hat and tangos over to greet her, lips already poised in a smooch pout.

EMMANUEL DISCOVERED WHAT he was put on this planet to do at the age of eight. His first public performance in his elementary school cafetorium was a revelation. As he finished a triple turn with a shoulder shimmy, the beaming stage lights set his white-and-orange suit ablaze. He felt himself radiate out from the stage to everyone in the audience. His schoolmates and teachers were all witnesses, and now they all knew. He was a singer, a performer, a natural artist.

He was doing his Juan Gabriel number, as flawlessly as Juan Gabriel himself. He stepped, swayed and shimmied, stepped swayed and shimmied, as he had done so many times across the living room with eyes fixed on the TV. He had wanted to get it just right.

But now with the stage, the lights, the music, the audience and this unnamable energy inside of him, Juan Gabriel's rhythms and beats became his. They belonged in his bones.

He closed his eyes and reached for the song he always kept inside of him like a secret he couldn't wait to share. Out it came, dancing up through him at his beckoning. It gathered strength as it pushed through his lungs and out his mouth into the microphone where it was transformed into a supernatural thing. Emmanuel was amazed. It blasted from the speakers with a life of its own.

And of course, he knew all the words like he knew his name and how to breathe.

"*Escucha esta canción que escribí para tí, mi amor,*" he sang as he slowly swept his arm over the audience, letting them know that this was for them, too.

He spotted his mother standing by the side entrance still wearing her work apron. She wiggled her fingers at him and mouthed "*Mijo*" with a wide smile. He wished his father could be there so he could see how good he was.

In class, Mrs. Medina had his classmates give him an ovation for his amazing performance and great courage. Outside during recess Joanna the popular girl and her friends invited him to play tetherball at their pole. As he swung the ball fiercely for the final kill, a group of three boys walked by and laughed. Some of Joanna's friends giggled too.

"What's so funny?" he asked, wanting in on the joke.

One of the girls answered, "Ricky says you dance like a *joto*."

FOR AS LONG as Emmanuel can remember, his mother always loved songs by Lucha Villa, Ednita Nazario, Las Jilguerillas and Paquita la del Barrio; larger-than-life Mexican women who bellowed into microphones like men and made their audiences squirm and blush during shows. Their big hands and knowing smirks filled his television screen. They used to scare him.

His mother would sing on Saturday mornings while the menudo brewed in the kitchen. Pedro Infante wept love songs on the radio she kept on the counter. Los Panchos harmonized sweet nostalgias. But before the melancholy could set in, his mother would split the air with Lola Beltrán's bellows and cries. She seemed unbreakable.

Her voice boomed and sparked like thunder and lightning through the house. Her back was very straight as she leaned her firm body at an angle, pointing like an arrow in the direction her wide-open mouth was sending her song.

He knew it shot straight up through the city smog and soared across, arching over the border and then down down down into some pueblo in Jalisco where it would find his father and strike him down dead. Dead. And Emmanuel would be glad for it.

THERE ARE MANY Mexicans who say that you can like Antonio Aguilar or Vicente Fernández, but you can't like both, and you certainly can't not like either one. Emmanuel disagreed. He never liked Antonio Aguilar or Vicente Fernández, which immediately put his Mexicano-ness into question. He found Vicente's mustache, his self-assured swagger overbearing. Antonio's cunning and degrading lyrics about women were completely unacceptable. Once, his cousin Chuy who was visiting from Tepatitlán jumped at the opportunity to bully him when Emmanuel casually informed him that he didn't care for Antonio or Vicente.

He tried provoking Emmanuel with a gruff smirk "What's up, primo? You're not Mexican anymore or what?" he drawled.

Emmanuel knew what he was getting at, the whole pocho-sell-out-thinking-you're-a-gringo-now-because-you-live-in-el-norte bit.

"I'm still Mexican. And what do you care anyway," he retorted. *Pendejo*, he thought. Since when was being a *ranchero* the only way to be a Mexicano? And besides, most of his family wasn't from the *charro*-loving *rancho* anyway, Emmanuel thought to himself.

Sensing he had effectively roused Emmanuel's spirit, cousin Chuy attempted to make nice with a special offer.

"*Vamos al Farallón*," he announced enthusiastically, stomping his ostrich-skin boot on the ground. "There's a shit-ton of cute girls there."

"I don't like clubs like that," Emmanuel answered sullenly.

"Come on! Let's go party. I'll even buy you a few drinks. Loosen you up a bit."

"I don't drink alcohol."

Chuy was getting impatient.

"I'll buy you a Coke."

Emmanuel shook his head.

"Come on, don't be a *pendejo*. What you need is to be around men more often instead of clinging to your mom's skirts all the time."

"Don't call me *pendejo, pendejo*. You don't know anything."

Emmanuel never liked listening to Antonio Aguilar or Vicente Fernández or watching them in movies because they made him think of his father. They made him imagine his father riding a great silver horse down lush green hillsides and through grassy valleys. He wore a tan-and-gold *charro* suit and a wide *charro* hat. His gold studs, buttons and buckles shone in the sun, and he smiled large white teeth through his dark mustache.

His horse knew the way to the little white adobe house. His father leapt off the horse and grabbed onto the tiny waist of the very young and pretty woman who waited for him outside. He swung her gleaming skirts into the cool darkness of the adobe house and disappeared. The word "Fin" would appear at the bottom of the frame.

Emmanuel hated thinking about it. He hated thinking about his father and this terrible fantasy, but he just couldn't help it. It always made him feel so lonely and unwanted. What was worse was when he felt like he was missing him, the man who'd left him and his mother without ever turning back to see if they were okay. Emmanuel could hardly remember him. In his mind, all he saw was Vicente Fernández.

"JUST LISTEN TO that, *mijo*." Emmanuel heard his mother call from the kitchen, suddenly enraptured amidst the orchestra of boiling pots and a humming radio.

The deep lament of Lola Beltrán's voice filled the glowing kitchen, rolling through the doorway and into the dining room with a melancholy as rich as the aroma of hot *pozole.*

His mother drifted toward him at the table, with Lola's lyrics filling her powerful lungs beneath her flowery dress.

"*Paloma negra donde andarás*" she sang as she placed his bowl in front of him.

"*Ya no jueges con mi honra parrandera, si tus caricias han de ser mías y de nadie más.*" He watched her wide mouth sing, drawing out the notes full of a pain and conviction he knew she kept behind her closed eyes.

"*Y aunque te ame, con locura, ya no vuelvas*" she slipped a small silver spoon into the chile saucer.

"*Eres la reja de un penal. Quiero ser libre y vivir con quien yo quiera,*" she moved the finely chopped coleslaw closer to his bowl and fixed her eyes on him. Her tired, knowing eyes that always reassured him that while life was hard, one could survive anything.

"*Dios dame fuerza que me estoy muriendo por irlo a buscar,*" she crooned the last words long and low, nodding her head gently to confirm their meaning.

She let out a deep sigh.

"She's not the queen for nothing," she finally said with a small smile as she shuffled her worn brown slippers back into the kitchen to bring her own bowl to the table.

Over time, Emannuel had noticed a change in his mother's singing. He couldn't quite pinpoint when it had happened, but something had shifted inside of her, unbeknownst to him. His mother's songs didn't boom anymore. They didn't shoot like arrows from her heart. They lingered now, moving gently through the house and eventually settling in the quiet shadows, amongst her dusty doilies and knitting bag. It made him uneasy.

"*Oiga mamá*, why don't you sing like you used to? Big and strong like Paquita la del Barrio?" He slurped the *pozole* from his spoon.

"No *hijo*. That is not strength. That is rage and bitterness. I don't want that anymore. Anger has a function. It helps us to move forward. But if you carry it too long, it'll knock you all the way down. I say, what's the point of carrying so much baggage if all you get to take to the other side is a fistful of dirt. *Un puño de tierra*. And even José José said it right, "*ya lo pasado, pasado.*"

What's in the past, is in the past. Emmanuel let the words sit and settle. He consulted with them, used them to turn the stale soil inside of him. What songs had remained dormant beneath, what songs should he bury below, put to rest, he pondered. The past. Emmanuel intended to put finally put it where it belonged.

JUAN GABRIEL FOUGHT back his tears as he stepped out the door into the cool dewy morning. His mother wept into her handkerchief.

"Don't cry mother. I'll be back soon with a lot of money. We'll have a big house and we'll never need anything again." He knelt to he ground at his mother's feet. She gave him his *bendición* and watched him disappear into the horizon.

A year later, the mailman handed her an envelope from her son. Enclosed was a thick wad of money and a letter. "Mother, this is for you so you can buy a television and watch me sing," Juan Gabriel wrote simply.

True to his word, Juan Gabriel was singing on *Siempre en Domingo*, the popular Mexican talent show that launched most of Latin America's most prominent singers into stardom. After months and months of scratching around for gigs in Juárez bars and dance clubs, he'd finally made it. This was his door to fame. No one had ever seen anything like him. His sensual pouting into the camera, his wild hips swinging in full 1970s spirit.

Emmanuel was inspired to the point of tears by Juan Gabriel's life story. He made it a point to watch the movie version of it whenever they'd show it on TV.

This wasn't a stiff *charro* with too many women and too much tequila. This was Juan Gabriel dressed neatly in collared, tucked-in shirts and well-tailored jackets, who sang with his heart, unafraid to show yearning and unadorned love. Heartbreak too. Juan Gabriel, who loved his mother more than anything and dedicated his triumphs to her, who didn't need a father to persevere.

Juan Gabriel didn't need *Sábado Gigante* or Don Francisco or the Estefans. He was a star on his own without the Miami Sound Machine. It was his irrepressible way of being himself and expressing his emotions that had made him into a comet that could not be stopped.

Emmanuel knew what he needed to do.

EMMANUEL FEELS HIS intestines knot and his jaws clench as the young woman chews on her lips and giggles nervously. Don Francisco strikes up the band.

The young woman tries to concentrate as Don Francisco begins to tango with El Chacal. She begins the song with a soft, quivering "*If I...*" that progresses steadily into a stronger, more confident and climactic "*AND AHEEE-IIIII...WILL ALWAYS...*" At the end, she finally fades off with a gentle and off-key "*...love youuuuuu.*" She even adds a small flourish with her dove-like hand. The trumpet remains quiet.

Don Francisco flings off El Chacal in a spin, swoops the ecstatic young woman up in his arms, almost hiding her with his enormous cowboy hat, and carries her off stage to await the next round. El Chacal holds his trumpet under his arm to applaud fiercely. The audience prepares for the next potential victim or winner.

Emmanuel wishes his mother were there somewhere in the audience to wiggle her fingers at him and say "*Mijo*, we're going to be fine." He wants someone to wish him the best instead of eagerly wait for him to be blasted by a bedazzled executioner or devoured by a man in a lion costume. But he knows she's at home sitting in front of the TV praying for him this very moment. Everyone is watching—his *tías*, his cousin from Jalisco, Juan Gabriel (maybe), that kid Ricky who called him a queer in elementary school, the entire San Gabriel Valley, the Estefans. His father.

Suddenly Emmanuel feels a rude tap on the shoulder and a quick shove toward the stage where Don Francisco is wearing a huge straw sombrero, already introducing him. Emmanuel Figueroa from El Sur de El Monte, California, with his interpretation of Juan Gabriel's "*Amor Eterno.*"

Without another thought, he surrenders to the blinding stage lights and to the music that starts up as soon as he steps onstage.

The audience, the cameras, even Don Francisco and El Chacal, despite their antics, dissolve into another world. Enveloped in pure sound and light, Emmanuel finds himself singing as he had done in the school talent show so many years ago, before he learned to be afraid, angry and resentful. He sings with his heart open for everyone to see. With every bit of the tenderness and sincerity he had learned from Juan Gabriel, and the strength and power from Lola Beltrán and his mother, he sings and dances because he knows that some things need to change in this world, like who calls the shots in music and TV. He sings because he knows so many things haven't changed or might never change, like drunken fathers, abandoned mothers and forgotten children. He balls up every bit of bitterness, anger, grief, doubt and fear into a single exploding note that rockets out of his body and leaves his being forever. He finishes what he has come to do.

Suddenly exhausted, he realizes El Chacal has not blown his trumpet, and that he's still a contender.

Don Francisco brings out the young woman, holding her very close by the waist. It's time for the audience to decide the winner, he announces.

"Karina Ochoaaaa!" He shouts into the microphone, raising and shaking her hand high in the air like a boxing champ. The crowd shouts and hoots, someone catcalls.

"Emmanuel Figueroaaaaa!" And now the crowd explodes in applause, stamping and screaming. There is no doubt, even the crowd knew he was the best.

Don Francisco smirks. *"Damas y caballeros la ganadora,* Karina OCHOAAAA!!!"

Don Francisco hugs the overjoyed young woman who begins to weep through her pretty, lipsticked smile. Her mother and sisters run onto the stage to celebrate, also weeping. The band strikes up a celebratory melody.

But the audience is not ready to celebrate. The crowd's commotion becomes disturbed with boos and thumbs down. They know who the real winner is. El Chacal dodges a flying cup. Waving at the deafening mass, Don Francisco pretends to laugh and tries to say something about this segment of *Sábado Gigante* being brought to you by Kraft and Palmolive. The winner's sisters and mother are still jumping up and down squealing, as El Chacal rocks side to side covering his ears through his hood.

As the chaos spreads, the lion leaps out suddenly from behind the gold streamers. The crowd screams as he flies past the girl, past El Chacal, just missing Emmanuel to land full force on Don Francisco.

A deafening silence of shock and horror descends on the studio.

Don Francisco lies unconscious with his microphone and straw sombrero strewn nearby. El Chacal, the producers and some on-site paramedics run to him. The crowd gasps, rising from their seats, and someone screams. The show cuts to blue on millions of TV screens around the world.

For the first time in its decades-long history, *Sábado Gigante* is cancelled for the evening.

Emmanuel and the young woman remain standing on the stage. She begins to cry, her pretty mascara streaming down her face, and is escorted off by her entourage of women. Emmanuel observes the entire scene, the fantasy come apart at the seams. The whole place could burn down, as far as he's concerned. He is sated, complete. *Ya lo pasado, pasado.*

INI Y FATI

~~~~~

YOU WOULD THINK that such an event, a bolt of lightning
shooting out of the sky to strike a little girl in a vacant lot,
would call immediate attention from the neighbors. But it did
not. Only the dogs pointed their snouts to the sky and howled.
Birds were startled into flight from their power line perches, but
even they quickly settled back to roosting in the stillness of a
late afternoon grown almost dark with pending rain. The sky
had become heavy and shadowed, a rare experience during those
years of drought when the blue sky imposed itself on the land
like a burden. But this year, the rain had returned, tenuously at
first and with much distrust, as if over the years it had lost faith
in the ground it was supposed to fall upon, and which it then
furiously pummeled with great reproach.

Fátima was playing in the plot of vacant land across the
street from her house when the lightning bolt knocked her body
flat to the ground. It was a block of still-undeveloped land, an
orphaned appendage to a large swath of new, two-storied homes
that frowned across at Fátima's street, where the houses sagged
and peeled, crouching humbly to the ground. Though the earth
was clotted with dried dirt and rocks, pocked with holes dug up

by rodents, she often played there alone until darkness called her back home.

Fátima was scouting the land, as she often did, for any new plants that had taken root or for animals that had died there since her last visit. Dutifully she checked on the various rotting corpses, noting their status, as if they were part of a garden she'd been charged with tending.

Fátima woke to an intense, warm light. She saw the light at first through her closed eyelids, saw the red glow of her illuminated membranes, as if a new bright day had risen around her. Slowly she blinked her eyes open, and indeed, the light was warm as it embraced her. Then she heard a voice stir from its depths.

"Fátima," the voice called her. "Fátima."

It was a sweet voice, one she did not recognize. From the light emerged a small face that peered out over Fátima's body with curiosity.

"You're okay now," said the young child, a round-cheeked face with dark eyes. The rest of the child emerged from the light, draped in a simple robe, which she gathered around her to crouch at Fátima's side.

"You're okay," she repeated. "See for yourself."

In the warm glow, Fátima stirred and inspected her body. She was still laid flat on the rocky earth but she felt no discomfort or pain, despite the thistles and jagged rocks. She looked again at the child who squatted at her side. She did not recognize the girl, who was younger than she was, and definitely smaller, though Fátima was not a particularly large child by any means. As she propped herself up, blinking her eyes wider and wider, Fátima began to realize the unfamiliarity of her situation, and her breath began to push faster, panicked, through her chest. She tried to look around but the light drowned everything out. The small child shuffled closer to her.

Shhhhh, she indicated with an index finger over her small pouty lips. "I told you you're okay now," she whispered. "Hey don't be scared," the child insisted. "The lightning can't harm you anymore. I saved you."

Fátima looked at the girl suspiciously. "Who are you? What am I doing here?"

"Well, you're still out here in the vacant lot, but you're safe now. I fixed you right up. It wasn't hard. Don't worry, I do it all the time. Well, I do it less now, you know, because people nowadays. Hey, you want to play something?"

"I don't know. I think I have to go home."

The young girl's face darkened and grew serious, the light that encapsulated her dimmed and receded. Fátima felt a stiff gust of cold wind graze the side of her body.

"Why?" the girl asked pointedly. "You're fine now. And it's not like they care," she gestured toward Fátima's house.

Fátima looked around as the bright halo receded further to reveal the neighborhood. She looked past the vacant lot to where her house stood forlorn and grey with a single dimly lit window. Curtains drawn, no one stirring.

Fátima frowned back at the girl, and inspected her more closely. What was this light coming from the girl, anyway?

"It's part of the halo," said the girl. "It's why you're alive," she added pointedly, flicking a tiny rock at Fátima's shoe.

Fátima flinched and drew her feet quickly under her, sitting up straight, alert, ready to spring into flight.

"It's not necessary," said the girl, twisting her mouth. "I told you already, you're safe now. It was just lightning."

Fátima inspected her hands, not a scrape to be found. She thought of her parents who would probably punish her if they found out what had happened. She knew they had no time or patience for any kind of trouble, especially not the lightning kind.

"Well, do you want to play or what?" Fátima finally asked.

The girl was digging up a rock with the tip of her blue satin slipper. She shrugged, seemingly disinterested, if not irritated.

"What's your name?" Fátima asked.

The girl inspected the sky and seemed to be listening to something far away. "My name? You can call me...Ini."

It seemed like the girl had just snatched that name out of one of the rain clouds, and Fátima frowned again. "Ini? Are you sure? I've never heard that name before."

"People call me by a lot of different names. And I don't like any of them. So I call myself Ini," she said, putting her fists at her hips. The halo had all but disappeared, and Ini seemed even smaller against the steel-colored sky. She also seemed indifferent to how out-of-place she appeared with her embroidered robes and curly blonde wig, upon which sat a tiny gold crown. For a moment, a severe silence settled in place of the gusts of wind from the coming storm. Fátima glanced over at her house again.

"Hey, I have something for you," Ini said with a brightness that startled Fátima. She produced from her robes two palm-size dolls made of woven grass reeds. "Here. This one's for you."

"Really?"

"I have many. Take it."

Fátima inspected the curious little doll. Unlike most dolls, this one seemed to wear pants and a T-shirt, and her grass hair was cut just above the shoulders, much like her own.

Ini floated her own doll down to Fátima's and greeted her in a high-pitched doll voice, "*¡Hola!*"

Fátima didn't know what to say.

"*¡Hola!*" Ini repeated.

"*Hola,*" Fátima's doll responded, solemnly.

"¿*Cómo te llamas?*"

"Fátima."

"Fátima? Are you sure? I've never heard of that name before."

Fátima caught on to the game.

"Yes, but you can call me Fati. What's your name?"

"Inocencia is my real name. But you can call me Ini for short. It's what my mother called me."

Fati sighed, let her guard down for once, and invited Ini on a tour of her garden.

ALMOST DAILY INI and Fati played in the vacant lot, regularly inspecting and tending to a garden no one else saw or cared about. Their dolls went on magical adventures in a landscape suddenly transformed from one of neglect into one of possibility, which Ini endowed with her special touch.

"Watch this," said Ini, and the thorny bush under which their dolls rested from their vigorous play suddenly bloomed with great purple flowers. Fátima gasped and watched in awe as buds appeared on the barren branches, swelling open to unravel their fleshy petals, stretching delicate necks toward patches of sunlight that broke through the dense clouds.

Fátima pushed her face into a cluster of blossoms and breathed in, deeply inhaling their sweet scent. She led her doll on an exploration of the magical bush.

Pleased, Ini's halo glowed.

Another day, they discovered a dead sparrow strewn among the rubble. Its tiny chest had been gashed open but it was otherwise intact, left to die alone under the unsympathetic sky. Fati crouched over the bird in perplexed silence. Though she'd seen many dead animals, most of them were at least half-eaten by their predator when she found them. She'd never seen a creature killed like this, not for food, but for some other reason she had not accounted for in nature.

"It's a common mistake," said Ini, "to think of animals as noble creatures. I remember my mother saying it all the time, that dogs were better than humans because they protected their young, and that was more than she could say for many people. But I can tell you animals are no better or worse than humans. And we are no better than they. They also take pleasure in killing."

Fati protested. "I don't kill things for fun. Most people don't."

"But we all sometimes do mean things for fun. There doesn't always have to be a reason, and we don't always have to care about being good or fair. Like crushing ants or spiders, or ripping petals off beautiful flowers. Sometimes it's just because."

Ini noticed Fátima holding her doll more tightly against her chest, as if to protect herself and the doll from the sparrow's fate.

"You're right. Most just do their best. We just want to feel protected and to protect people we love, right? There's nothing wrong with that. Right?"

IT HAD BEEN a very long time since Ini had gone out of her way to befriend another girl, let alone a living one. Many years ago, she had heard of another child martyr who'd been preserved to near perfection and was now a very popular attraction in the big city's cathedral. She'd gone there herself one day just to see what all the excitement was about. And for other reasons.

It had taken her many many years to finally get around to making the annoying trek to the city from her hometown. She'd traveled across the sierra down into grasslands that fed into the patchy suburbs skirting the old metropolis. The city had changed much since the first time she'd visited, back when she was still alive, a little girl clinging to her father's sleeve as they moved through the crowded rush of people. How vulnerable she'd been, so much that she'd cling to the man who would hurt her and end her life. But now she made her way alone and unafraid through the cobblestone streets, guided by the familiar old buildings that now crumbled in the quaking thrust of modernity. The cathedral had been easier to find back then as it towered well above any other building and imposed itself on the land and everyone on it far and wide—small people who lived as if to bow before its absolute, macabre authority. Now, it seemed to Ini, the cathedral stood almost lost among high-rise buildings, corporate offices' glittering glass surfaces. And yet, its gravity could still be felt as it continued to draw streams of believers.

Ini walked past the beggars and the sick, the disfigured and the dismembered as they moaned their pleas. The same timeless songs of the disconsolate. This would never change, she knew. The most wretched things never do. And so long as this suffering continued to exist, so would she, patroness of the miserable. She existed because of them and for them. And, of course, because of her own suffering. She'd come to realize this, little by little, over the centuries. Ini followed the line of the devout that shuffled along, resigned to their wait. She walked past them to the long glass box on its altar, flanked by flowers and fruits, letters, drawings, garlanded by rosaries.

She saw that the girl lay dressed in a white communion dress. Paper-thin, her skin had begun to crack. Her nostrils were plugged with small, bunched-up scraps of gauze, as it was said that blood sometimes seeped from the orifices. Her worshippers would weep aloud and sing songs at the sight of the blood. Ini envied the girl for still having a body, even a decaying one. At least it was her own. Most of all, she envied the devotion showered upon her inert body by the believers.

Ini's body had been bludgeoned irreparably and not enough had remained for pilgrims to gather around. Instead, a large doll had been made in her likeness, or that's what they claimed. But Ini knew it was way off, and not by accident, not just in small details. She was not blonde in life, nor did she have glossy curly locks. Her face was neither smooth nor fair. She'd been pockmarked and scratched, the color of clay. And she certainly did not have blue eyes, not even close. She remembers how dark they were, two small polished stones. She remembers thinking her eyes could protect her, like amulets, or like two tiny weapons she could throw at someone and draw blood, at least a little.

Now she was a ceramic doll wearing a wig made of another child's hair. Her clothes were crafted from fine fabric, carefully stitched and embroidered satin, blue to match her new eyes.

Ini studied the girl in the glass box for signs of life.

But the girl lay unresponsive and unstained by blood, looking like a lousy papier-mâché job. If she were strung up and beaten like a piñata, she'd be the most disappointing kind, Ini thought. She reread the plaque at the base of the altar for details about the nature of the girl's death, and found nothing but generic information about being "murdered by her own father." She scoffed, "What virgin saint wasn't 'murdered by her own father?'" Ini was unimpressed, impatient as ever. She hadn't really come here for stains or miracles. She came here to talk.

"Well, I'm here," she said to the girl. But the girl remained silent, frozen in her death box.

"Can't you see, I'm like you. I came all the way here to visit you."

Still the girl did not speak.

It was then that Ini understood. There was nothing and no one else to talk to about their purpose, about who they were, about their girl lives cut too short. She had found only silence, and in it she was just another story of death and decay. And now that she had time, all of eternity from the looks of it, there was no one but herself to consult in her solitude. She saw nothing in the other virgins, saints and martyrs she'd visited. No sign of God to be found. And so she resorted to what she did have. She became a student of mortals, in whom she attempted to see her own reflection. Her pilgrims became her endless, fractured mirror. It was the best she could do.

And now, in this place so far from home, she became a student of Fátima. Unexpectedly, she saw a version of herself in Fati that was so clear, it was as if she were watching herself, alive in this time. How strange that people and circumstances could remain so much the same after all the years that had passed. And because of it, as she watched Fati wander across the street from her home to the vacant lot and then bound over the broken, unwanted land as if she were a deer released into a meadow, Ini felt a great swelling desire to protect her. As their days of play continued, this need to shield Fati from a looming fate sharpened fiercely with her impetuous child's love, as deep as it was mercurial.

87

FÁTIMA AND INI were playing when a small pack of boys walked by. They bounced a worn basketball, rhythmically slamming its leathery face against the asphalt with loud thuds that echoed throughout the street. Fati groaned. One of them was a boy who without fail went out of his way to offend or humiliate her. As usual, without provocation, reason or hurry, he steered the group of boys toward Fati. Ini noted how the boys seemed to share a single mind for mischief. They were propelled by a shared hunger for violence. She watched Fati focus hard on her doll as she sat on the ground and tried to ignore the approaching pack.

"Hey Fati!" the boy called, wearing an expression that Ini recognized. He was the first to pick up a small white stone and fling it at Fati, chuckling. He missed. "Hey Fatty! Hey Footsie! Hey Foochi! Foochi, foochi coochi!" he and the boys sang.

"Aw, dumb fat, foochi coochi Fati playing with baby dolls." He threw another stone. It landed near Fati's hand before she pulled it away. The boys laughed as they looked around for their own stones to fling. Foochi coochi they repeated among themselves through their mouthfuls of rotten teeth and sputtering saliva.

Fati knew the best she could do was always to ignore them, or as in this case, get away as quickly as possible. She stood up, looking for the best escape route, but Ini took hold of her arm and smiled coolly.

The boy dropped his stones and began to whimper, then broke into a groan as he swatted at his legs, deliberately at first, then frantically, while his posse looked on in confusion. He screamed for help. Fati looked more carefully and saw that his pant legs were covered in red ants. They swarmed toward his crotch, up toward his torso. He dropped to the ground enveloped in ants, and rolled, as if they were flames. Ini and Fati watched. Then, without a word, they migrated to a more peaceful part of the lot where they could continue with their blameless play.

INI WAS IN an especially good mood. She asked Fati dozens of questions about her day, complimented the buttons on her sweater, tried to call her attention to the dead groundhog she'd found. She sang a song as she played with her doll, flying it in the air as if it were a tiny airplane.

But Fati was immersed in a sullen mood and did not reciprocate. She pretended to ignore her and played alone, sorting stones into different piles, though their categories were still ambiguous. Round rocks, sharp rocks, red-brown rocks, grey rocks, rocks with shiny specks in them. Rocks that look like faces, rocks that work like logs. Rocks good for cutting, rocks good for stacking. She didn't know yet.

She was taking inventory of all the unusual events she'd witnessed in the last couple of weeks since she'd met Ini. Fati considered the blooming bush, the resuscitated sparrow, but mostly she thought about the boy who'd since recovered from the ant attack and returned to school. She had learned that he had suffered through days of very high fever, in addition to the countless painful welts that had swollen his entire body. He could hardly breathe and had to go to the emergency room. Now that he'd returned, he was different, noted Fati. Instead of joyously insulting her as he'd always done when they crossed paths, he now avoided eye contact and quickly moved away.

And there'd been another incident. Fati had invited a friend to join her and Ini, but somehow she had fallen off her bike as she arrived to the vacant lot. Fati had not seen her since. When Fati went to visit, her mother said something about a broken leg and sent Fátima away with a bitter glare.

Ini landed her doll on one of Fátima's pile of stones. "Did you like my song? My mother taught it to me when I was a little child."

"But you're still a child," Fati pointed out.

Ini paused and turned to Fátima. "Yes. And no."

And then Ini told her a story. She knew Fati had wanted to ask. It was about how her own father had killed her a long time ago. She tells her about how she was made into a virgin saint, a child martyr. She explains how hard it is to be this thing that people worship, grovel before, make offerings to. But she's accepted her fate, she tells Fati, and what's more, she's learned that she doesn't have to do anything she doesn't want to do.

"I'm more picky now about what miracles I do. I used to try to fix every broken arm and cure every sickness the pilgrims laid at my feet. I'd hear them with every candle they lit. I liked the flowers they brought me, the gold charms they hung at my altar. I guess I liked the attention."

"But now I just don't see the point anymore. What's in it for me? I mean, I still fulfill my duties, I stand there for all the people, let them take me on tour when they want. You'd be surprised by how much I travel. The farther away people go, the farther I travel too. It can get exhausting. Actually, that's why I'm here in the first place." With her chin she gestured to a house down the street. "Your neighbors brought me here all the way from my hometown. I guess folks need a lot of help around here. I went out for some fresh air and that's when I found you here."

Fati studied Ini's small body perched on a fallen tree, walking her doll along its cracked and rotted trunk. To her, Ini seemed like a fragile thread caught between the enormous menacing sky and the jagged landscape. In fact, she was. Or at least she had once been. It was hard to know how fragile Ini really was. After all, she had powers. It occurred to Fati how awful and hard it must be to be a child martyr. It must have been scary to get stabbed to death by her own father.

Maybe Ini was not bad after all, Fátima thought. She felt regret for having suspected her of wrongdoing. After all, kids fall off bikes all the time. Insect bites are nothing out of the ordinary. It seemed silly to start blaming things on a virgin saint just because you happen to know one, let alone one that had suffered such violence as Ini.

Fati thought about her own father. He would never do such a thing, she thought, but then she remembered all those times she was sure he'd kill her mother. Even when it was her mother holding the sewing scissors, she thought it would be her dad who'd do the killing. She feared for her mother during those panicked moments. And without her, who's to say he wouldn't come after her or her siblings? Where else would he direct all that rage he brought home with him from work, that he carried balled up in his hard, caved-in chest and unleashed upon her mother?

Fati shook these thoughts from her mind. She noticed Ini had reorganized her stones and stacked them into an impossible tower. Ini had also been watching her, pensively, but said nothing.

That night, Fati kept as far away as she could from her father. From a distance, she watched him with brooding attention.

IT'S HARD TO see the mothers behind their veils. They are shielded, hidden, silenced by the fathers, whose voices echo in all the throats, choke up the hallways of the house with their reverberations so that even when they are not there, even in their absence, the walls are like an extension of their tyrannical bodies.

Some mothers are as transparent as curtains held up against the light. Their purpose is to shield or to frame another scene with their bodies. Out there, my daughters, they seem to say. Out there is a place to go, behold the unknown. What is a mother if not a frame to show you what you may become, or what you must avoid?

Ini's mother had been long gone. Even while Ini was alive, her mother was already just a handful of memories. Without a curtain to shield, protect or even frame, Ini saw nothing of her future except her father, his imposing body, the shape of a fist taking up the volume of an entire room, which in truth, was the entire house, as there was only one room. And now, nearly two centuries later, she had only faceless memories of her mother. Only ideas transplanted from the flickering images of so many veiled mothers who had kneeled before her, lighting candles and laying offerings at her feet. Desperate mothers, whispering their needs and wishes, Ini wasn't sure if these women truly believed she was listening, so consumed were they in shaping their pleas into soft streams of air, like fingers running so quickly over rosary beads they turn the strings to water. But Ini did listen. She watched them, studied them with intense curiosity through her painted glass eyes and listened to them speak about their desperate lives.

Desperation: She knew how it could drop women to their knees, drop them dead even. Or it could prop them up, possess them, send them off into a blind battle, transform their limbs into an impossible armament, conjure unbidden blades into their hallucinating hands until all blood had been spent and the battle, their battle, was over. On foot or on their knees, the result was often the same—drop dead. It had been so for her mother and had been so for her as well. In the end, their fates had been the same. Dead. Except not. Except Ini was here, a virgin saint, a child martyr, as they called her, and a performer of miracles. She was holy, eternal, and a monster, or so she believed sometimes. She had no way of finding her mother, who became more lost to her with every passing year. And yet, Ini persisted, despite her powerlessness in the face of forces she did not understand. She persisted because of her powers. Though she didn't know where they came from, or why she'd been endowed with them, she knew they were hers, ever since the fateful day of her human body's death so long ago, and they would continue to be hers until the end of time.

AT THE END of their play, after they said their unceremonious goodbyes, Ini always watched Fati trot back home and reappear on the other side of the front window. By evening, the curtains were usually parted and Ini could catch glimpses of Fati's family life played out under the light bulb. Ini watched Fati's mother with fascination, and when the curtains were drawn shut, she often recognized her shadow when it appeared in the window frame like the portrait of a ghost. Her movements were like a slow dance, as if she were underwater and sometimes coming up for air, craning her neck up to the light bulb, gasping. A long neck, surely once beautiful, a delicate thing to behold. Ini watched her fighting the

93

invisible current, the daily, round-the-clock battle of domesticity that by evening time left her worn and breathless. She also watched her struggle against the crashing waves of the father's temperament. She watched her slowly drown while swimming as fast as she could. Ini saw her sink, but every time she touched bottom, Ini knew that somewhere, just outside the frame of the window, there was little Fátima, waiting among the sand and stones to push her mother back up. It occurred to Ini that children could be both burdens and buoys. They could be the ground on which an endless journey was marked, or the earth on which to stand and grow tall. She tried not to wonder which one she'd been. It was too late for that.

IT BECAME OBVIOUS to Fati that Ini had something on her mind. She'd noticed Ini muttering to herself while shielding her play with her back turned to her. She didn't even have her doll with her.

It didn't take long for Ini to get to the point. She had something to propose to Fati. It was a very special favor she'd rarely granted in all of her holy years, she said.

Fati listened very seriously, trying to think of what favor she might need that Ini had to offer. It made her nervous.

Ini cleared her throat. "If you'd like, I could get rid of your father. Then you and your mom and siblings wouldn't have to worry about him again."

Fati was completely confused. "Get *rid* of him? Like how? Like, make him disappear into thin air?" She felt panic rise inside of her.

But Ini remained cool. She'd given this plenty of thought. "Believe me, if I'd been given the opportunity I'm giving you, I would have taken it. But I was alone with no one to protect me. Now you have me. It's my job to protect."

But Fati could not imagine getting rid of her father, not into thin air, not in a vat of acid, not stuck in the middle of a train crossing, not falling off a very tall ladder, not severed to pieces in a terrible car accident.

Ini smiled, "You'd be surprised what people ask for, what they really want in their hearts. I can see it. Nothing alarms me now."

"What about God? Isn't it wrong to get rid of someone? A sin, a crime?"

Ini had known she would ask this, as they all eventually do. "What *about* God?"

"Well, do you know him? Do you get to see him? Wouldn't he punish you or us for doing something like that?" She had so many questions she didn't know where to start.

"God? Oh. Nothing. I know nothing about him, or whatever that is. At least not any more than you."

"But you're holy. You make miracles. You don't know anything at all?"

"I know what I know. And that's that no God has ever talked to me. I've received no revelations. Except, of course, myself. This thing I that I woke up as one day is the revelation. I am what I am with no explanation at all, just like when I was a real girl, just like you. There's no explanation for any of it."

Fátima became flustered. "But if you exist, then there must be a God," she insisted.

"Why? Why must there be a God?" Ini snapped. "Why can't we just exist, on our own, for no other reason than to exist for our own sake?"

"But then we'd be all alone. With no one to look after us, no one to protect us. There would be no point to anything, nothing would make sense."

"*We* look after ourselves. *We* protect each other. People come to me because they've given up on God. They look to me to protect them. But what can I protect them against? The true source of their despair is each other. The true sins are the ones they commit against each other, not against some judging god. Sure, I can perform some miracles, but in the larger scheme of things, even in the small lives of those I help, it's really nothing at all. I mend peoples' petty ailments, and for what? So they can go back to living their miserable lives. Full of hunger, abuse, disaster. And yet, people insist on living."

Fati had fallen silent. She sat on a large slab of broken concrete that jutted from the ground like the ruins of an ancient civilization.

"In truth, the sooner we do away with God, in the all-powerful, all-knowing Holy Father sense, the better off we'll be. Think about it, Fati. What have the all-powerful fathers gotten us anyway?"

"Think about it," Ini instructed again and disappeared herself into thin air without another word.

FATI OPENED HER front door to behold the storm-punished landscape. The old rickety houses on her block swelled with the humidity. The rain had conspired with termites and other vermin that had been laboring with enduring patience through the seasons. The new houses, for all their pretentions, were soggy as well, their soft interiors had already begun to molder and fall apart. Their foundations trembled as rainwater found weaknesses to wear on, giving the earth permission to shift and wash away. Old and new, the houses clung tenuously to the earth as a new storm gathered. It had already begun its steady march from the horizon.

Ini was waiting for her in the vacant lot, as usual. Without a word they accepted the storm's arrival and let it beat down on them as it pleased. The girls found their thorny bush, abundant with its purple flowers that had not stopped blooming since Ini had brought them forth. They crawled under it and nestled in a bed of blossoms whose scent, both pungent and sweet with flowers in various states of decay, enveloped them. Before long, the insistent rain pushed through the web of branches to find them. It broke apart the dirt beneath their folded bodies and water streamed around them, pulling at their ankles. Ini and Fati held each other tightly, anchoring themselves with heads butted together. The rain drenched Ini's robes and began to pull the wig from her porcelain head. Muddied, her satin shoes were no longer sky blue. Fati, made of solid flesh, muscle and bone, shielded Ini's small head beneath her chin. She pulled her little body against her own, so that Ini could curl onto her lap. She picked her up and cradled her in her arms, rocking her. She found the words to a lullaby she'd forgotten about and sang them to Ini until she fell asleep.

NEW FIRE SONGS

〜〜〜〜

WE'D MEANT FOR the balloon to rise penis-first with the large pink balls pushing up from below, like the big fuck-you it was supposed to be. Instead, the balls rose like a rubbery cloud that scraped through the gnarled tree canopy with the phallus pointed straight down. But it was a miracle it didn't tear on the pointed walnut branches, so our disappointment dissolved as we saw our pink balloon rise into the vast cloudless sky. We howled laughing. It was their balloon now.

With nothing in its way, the pink balloon, about the size of a small cow, went up and up. The farmers ran from their white wooden houses, rifles ready, and tried to shoot it down with no success. We saw their wives peeking from behind the curtained windows. Then they brought out one of their sons, a taller and leaner but otherwise identical version of themselves, to fly a drone up there, but it merely nudged the thing along. The penis rose slightly and was picked up by a wind current and continued, re-energized, on its way. Throughout the following day, the penis-shaped balloon drifted over the flat land, over farms and their various configurations of crop.

Eventually, the penis wilted and shriveled and finally got caught on a tall eucalyptus tree near the highway where a murder of crows had taken roost. The birds picked at its flaccid rubbery flesh but then abandoned it when their interest ran out. The farmers watched the scrappy pink skin hang limply for all of the neighboring farmers to see, though out of respect their neighbors cast their eyes to the ground or squinted away. The farmers clenched and unclenched their pink-white fists, baring their teeth as they talked to one another, their faces also like fists, open-closed, drained of blood in identical pallor.

We watched from the forest of ancient walnut trees where we live. We've been here so long that we've grown defiant. We dare the farmers to burn the grove, we send them mocking messages. They could burn their own legacy, the names of their own grandfathers, but they are not ready to make this sacrifice for the sake of getting to us. They could probably plow the trees down, one by one, but we know that only fire will sate their rage. But they are unfamiliar with such rites, and the idea frightens them. Fire rituals are so pagan, and they've left all of that far behind. Their great great greatest ancestors may have been comfortable with it back in the day, but they were Christians now, had been for generations, and practiced newer rituals. Now they were more comfortable with water, and they would fight for it with all of their blood if necessary, since they knew that their blood was bound up with the water. It was their livelihood. Ever since they arrived in this land, they'd understood the extent to which this was and is true. Water was everything. It was even in the Bible. Jesus Christ and all his people talked about water, water as a living thing. Baptisms in water gave them new life. Christ had walked on water. He bled water and blood when he was pierced with a lance as he hung on the cross.

They needed water to grow their crops. They had to get it at any cost. Water is what fed the ancient walnut groves, what made them grow tall and strong. Those trees had been the pillars of their farm, had raised it to prominence, had enabled their family and their kin to be fruitful and multiply.

Over time, the farmers moved on to more profitable crops and eventually stopped watering the groves. But the trees continued to grow green and tall. They continued to bear fruit, though the family no longer collected it. Their roots learned to reach deep into the earth, finding the water for their thirst. The trees grew self-sufficient. They dropped their own seeds, gave birth to their own saplings, pushing them up from the shaded dirt toward the light that cut and laced the canopy above.

Then we moved in, and like the trees, we thrived. But we, the young ones, hungered for the light.

BEFORE THE WALNUT grove, many of us had started at the vineyards. Green globes of grapes nestled among heavy garlands of leaves, patiently grew fat, turning the color of blood on their vines. Some of our elders still know the stories about when the vines were once but tender, crushable things strung over a few sticks and wire. Now the vines were woody and thick, like the trunks of trees. The elders never wondered what would have happened if we had crushed the farmers' vines, snapped the necks of their saplings while we still could. There probably wouldn't be a walnut grove, at least not for us, we figured. So where would we be now? Where would the farmers be? These days we wondered mostly among ourselves. The elders would not speak of it. They kept the fire and fanned away our questions with thick coils of smoke, sucking on their toothless gums. But we, the young ones, whispered these questions among ourselves as we stabbed the black earth with twigs and watched the farmers go about their routine days.

We've learned to memorize every one of their movements, as regular as the sun. They are as bound to its rhythms, to the will of the earth, as we are. It's the one thing we have always shared in common. From a distance, we can see that in this way, we are quite the same. From the shelter of the grove, we see how vulnerable they are, but also how great is their hatred for us.

From our youngest days, as babies, our mothers sang rhymes about the farmers to us. They taught us to carefully mind the farmer at every instant, as it is essential to always know where they are and what they are doing. We sang these songs to ourselves as young children playing in the dirt. We sang the grape songs, and we sang walnut songs. We even sang cotton songs because we all came from different farms before the grove, and from other places before that. The work songs are very old, of course, and we no longer know what it's like to work in the fields like that, crouching over the crop, crouching under the sun, bowing under the duster as it flies overhead. Working until you raise your face to the uninterrupted sky to steal a final breath. Those days are over. Now we, the younger ones, try to make up new songs but all we have are strange wordless songs that we beat out of the ground with sticks, with our feet and fists.

BEFORE LONG, IT became clear to us that our penis-balloon prank had profoundly disturbed the farmers, from way down in the depths of their primordial subconscious to the very top of their well-aware minds. Between the bodies of trees, we watched the farmers' faces alight as if they were discovering fire for the first time. They were learning to reclaim that side of their heritage, taking up torches, lighting them afire. They found new life, a hidden life they'd not known, in gathering under the sky and lighting one another's flames. They came to know one another's faces, eyes made more alive in the flickering torch. In this new-found intimacy, something warmed and stirred.

One afternoon, almost as if by accident, the way they'd discovered fire, they learned to sacrifice an animal. Perhaps they did it first to scare us, then because it pleased them. We watched them take a squirrel and shred it. But almost immediately they saw how small its organs were, not much more than a handful of guts, its crudely skinned fur as ugly as a hastily shaved mustache. They realized it was not worth it. By the next evening, they acquired a large possum that someone's kid brought in. The following night he brought a raccoon. He showed it to them by the light of a nascent bonfire as he held it out by the legs, blood dripping from its snout. At first the farmers hesitated as he offered them the creature, holding it out before them like the offering it was. Had he been out hunting these creatures the whole time? They seemed to wonder, glancing at each other. They consulted the shadows that waved like dark flags, emblems of their own emerging desires.

Yes, he had. We knew. And other things. We'd seen him.

But finally, the farmers accepted the strange gift from the earnest young man. By the next evening they'd learned to accept the kill without hesitation or doubt. The father disemboweled it, raked out its innards with a garden tool. They made interesting displays of the quartered animal. The women hung its organs from a frame, propped it up with rocks and dirt. Then they lit a fire. We watched quietly. We were not unfamiliar with the gutting of various animals, though we would have barbecued the thing and sliced off its sizzling flesh onto warmed tortillas and topped it off with chile sauce and a squeeze of lime. We would have thanked the little creature for giving our families nourishment. But we understood that they were working on a symbolic level. We saw it stirring, growing stronger as it flickered on their faces.

What was most clear was that they knew we were watching them. This show was for us.

I WILL NOT speak about the fate of our boy, we do not speak of these things except among ourselves, as we do not speak to others about our most sacred things. But I will say that we should have been more cautious. We should have known that their little hunter would be waiting for one of us to stray, as our boy did. He'd ventured to the far edge of the grove, much farther than we were supposed to go.

That night, when the wails had died down and darkness gripped the grove, we gathered among the roots of the oldest and largest tree. The elders had called us to discuss what had taken place. We'd been unable to recover our boy, and our elders were enraged, desperate in a way we'd never seen them before. Around the smallest, dimmest fire, the elders reproached us furiously. They had warned us, and we had defied their will.

They demanded answers from us, though we had very little information, practically nothing to add to what was already known about what had transpired. Our boy had acted alone, perhaps carried away by fun or emboldened by our earlier displays of bravado. He'd gone too far, trespassed beyond the edge. He was going to play another prank on his own, but he'd been caught. The farmers' hunter boy had been waiting for this opportunity.

In the flickering light, the elders hissed at us and proceeded to whisper among themselves so as not to attract more attention from the farmers, who would soon be gathering again near the edge of the grove. The elders were not diminished by the darkness this tragedy had cast upon us, but rather, they grew more strong and muscular as they spoke. It reminded us that somewhere far back in our lineages, we'd once been warriors. Warriors of the sierras, warriors of the lowlands, warriors of the desert and warriors of the jungle. We were not always just crop gatherers or tree squatters, not always slaves or runaways.

That night, the farmers gathered too, with their fire and their animal sacrifice. Like us, they were also quiet. Instead of the loud grunts they'd recently learned to coordinate into gruff chants, they whispered among themselves, as if they were listening for us, waiting for us. But we did not dare to go and look out at them. We sat still, withering beneath the reproachful glare of the elders, feeling the rumble of the farmers' feet shifting around their fire as it hungrily licked the black sky. The walnut branches crackled with their hushed talk.

It was understood, inside the grove and out, that in our silence and their listening, a true hunt had now begun.

The elders informed us that they would meet separately to decide on how to proceed. They warned us to not take any action, we'd done enough.

But youth boiled in our dark blood. It could not be helped.

105

THE BLAZE WAS enormous, shooting into the black sky. For a great while, there was a vast silence all around, a great listening, though the fire grew tall and danced like a god's tongue, speaking a language that no one knew. But we understood. We saw the fire grow larger as we roused everyone from their sleep, hurried them to grab their small belongings and their babies. The elders already stood at the edge of the grove, resigned, witnessing an end they had known would come.

We ran, we ran, out of the grove and into the fields, seeking cover in shadows so as to not meet the farmers as they also fled. We knew they'd surely come after us now. But some of us paused to contemplate the look of horror and rage in the farmers' eyes, to see how this night's fire shone on their faces.

The farmhouse was alive with fire. Indeed, a towering tongue, it sang to the heavens as shots rang, as screams rose.

A fire, a fire! Runrunrun! We start our lives anew! The words came to us as we ran. We were already singing the new songs as we vanished into the night.

ME MUERO

~~~~~

EVERYONE'S MOMENT COMES eventually. In my case, my moment is now. Right now. The separation is taking place, I am peeling back from myself. This tension I feel tugging between the two is my fear. I could make this very difficult for myself or I could just let go. I choose to not fear the inevitable and I feel the tension dissolve, it melts away smoothly and I peel away gently. I let go of the last point of connection without a bit of grief. That's it. Once you get past the hard part, dying is not difficult at all.

I lie here alone on the cement floor of the patio, the same as before though everything is different now. This is my body and this is me.

I'd timed it just right, when I found myself alone out on the patio. Before long, one by one, a few of my cousins had begun to walk over to take a look at my body before retreating back into the house. The kids whispered too loudly to be discreet, all in a bunch at the door, inquiring from the threshold. They shoved one another to see my body. Finally an uncle approached me, crouching down to touch my wrist, my neck. I watched him as he inspected my face, looking into my vacant eyes, squinting a little, like peering through the tinted windows of a parked car. He turned back to the inquisitive crowd inside and shook his head. They understood. Now that the wait was over, they dispersed, everyone back to their respective business of food, talk and play. One or two at a time, they stepped into the patio's quietude and leaned ever so slightly to bear witness to the fact that I was truly dead. Only their shadows touched me.

By now, my mother must know I am dead, too.

I decide to get up, out of my body. I know there are things that need doing. I can't just go away, not yet. I leave my body there on the ground to go and find out what there is to be done.

My aunts, uncles and cousins are circulating in the house. I feel my family shifting, moving like weather over the earth. The rumbling of busy *tías* loaded down with thick bodies and domestic duties. The rain of young children in chase. The uncles, mountains that won't lift a finger here except when drunk, to dance or fight. I make my way through the house looking for cousins who don't seem to notice me as I brush past them in the hallway, nor do my aunts when I walk into the kitchen where they're sorting out pans and dishes. No one sees me or hears me.

I sigh, I hum, I clear my throat, I utter sounds, but no one responds to me. I find my mom listening to some *tías* gossiping in the living room. *Mami?* But she doesn't hear me. Ma. She looks somber, but I can tell she's just trying to be polite and sociable with my *tías* by appearing to at least be listening to them. *Mamá.* She turns and stares through me to the back door. I don't know what to do. I touch her arm, her face, but she does not respond. I hadn't really considered this before, so consumed was I with the busy, painful undertaking of dying. But now I wonder, suddenly panicked, what if I can't talk to my mother ever again? Or my siblings, or my father? What if I can't talk to anyone ever again? I don't know what is going to happen to me after my body is gone, or what I'll do, or for how much time. For once, for the flash of an instant, the prospect of this new solitude frightens me.

BY THE TIME I return to the patio, a loose circle of men have gathered around my body. My uncles, cousins and their friends stand around it chatting and sipping on their Cokes and Budweisers. Occasionally they glance down at my body while they talk soccer matches and Teamster gossip. I hear the voices of the women inside the house getting loud, laughing and shouting as they prepare food for the children and the men. It would be a lot warmer in the kitchen if the kids didn't leave the door open every time they ran in and out of the house. The women flip tortillas on the hot grill and stir spoons into sauces and stews. They take turns going outside, carrying steaming bowls and small baskets of hot tortillas to the husbands and sons who are still talking about soccer. Beside them, my body is still lying there on the white cement. Everyone is careful not to step over it.

I don't mind that my body is lying there. The concrete is flat and dry, mostly smooth and dotted with many tiny holes where the wet cement air bubbles used to be. The day is overcast in that Southern California way, the sky colorless with the sunlight diffused through a thin cloud cover. Fortunately, the heat has been kept at bay, which is a good thing for my fully exposed body. But the most important thing is that the ground is very clean. My aunts sweep the patio thoroughly and often. Only a few flower buds and leaves from the avocado tree litter the ground. No dirt or insects to disturb me.

DESPITE HAVING NEVER been dead before, not even having had an out-of-body experience as some living people claim, I have a feeling that if I tried, I could figure out how to make my family members hear, see and feel me. This was hard enough when I was alive, but certainly it requires new strategies now. I leave my body again and go back into the house. I say "Hey," to my cousin Cristina who happens to be walking by, just to see what happens. Nothing happens. She keeps walking without acknowledging me. Then I see my cousin Danny walking toward me, so I decide to try speaking more loudly.

I say "Hey," and he pauses, turns around, like he thought he heard someone call his name. I get right in front of his face, and take a good look at his eyes buried under the dense bar of his brow. The bones in his face have thickened considerably since I last remember him, when he was a chubby boy crowned in golden curls. We were born only a month apart and raised together all our lives, but it's only now that I really notice he has become a man. I look more closely and there, I see it. He's still the same Danny. But my cousin doesn't see me and continues on his way.

It's really not very different from being alive, actually. I see it happen all the time, someone will say something but no one will hear them, mostly because they didn't really believe anyone would in the first place. They are startled when someone happens to catch what they said.

I want someone to hear me. The house is full of cousins, and I pick one. I see my cousin Alex and walk toward him and say "Hey, Alex." He turns around and looks at me and says, "Oh hey, what's up, cuz?" I smile at him and shake my head. "Nothing," I say quietly now, relieved.

Mami? I find my mother again. She is watching over the toddlers rambling around the living room.

"*Mamá?*"

"*Mija,*" she responds looking relieved to see me. "*Dónde andas?*"

"*Buscándote. Y esperando terminar esto. Mámi, no has salido a ver mi cuerpo.*"

"*Para qué, mija? Eso es lo de menos. Es el puro cascarón.*"

"*Es cierto. Tienes razón. Pero tengo que atenderlo hasta que termine.*"

"*Mija, solo tú sabes cómo hacer estas cosas como se debe. En esto no te puedo ayudar mucho.*"

"*Pues poco a poco voy viendo como. Y aprendiendo.*"[1]

I know she knows it is not necessary to come outside to see me because that part of me will be taken care of. It is not really the part that matters the most to either of us. I know she knows I will deal with it appropriately and she's letting me do as I see fit. I am no longer afraid.

I want to lie in my body again for a while and be still for a bit to think. I don't want to sit on the couch in the living room next to the kids playing Xbox, or at the breakfast bar in the kitchen near the women, my aunts' tireless chatter and the noise of kitchen equipment. I go back outside to where the men are standing around my body, more empty beer cans set on the ground. I lie down in it again without disturbing their

---

1 *Mija,* where have you been?

    Looking for you. And waiting to finish all of this. You haven't gone outside to see my body.

    What for? That's the least important part. It's just a shell.

    You're right. But I still have to tend to it until it's all done.

    My daughter, only you know how it's to be done. I can't help you much in this.

    Well, little by little, I see how. I am learning.

conversation. It feels like when I was a very little girl and I'd sit in a huge cardboard box, playing house by myself, with just enough privacy to unfold my quiet musings.

But now, resting here inside my body it's like I'm lying in a shoebox without a lid, or at the bottom of a canoe watching the clouds drift above. I see some black wires cutting across the sky. Some pigeons clean and fluff their feathers.

NOW THAT I'VE figured out that I can get people to hear and see me, I exchange some words with whomever I run into. I make small talk here and there, ask the kids about their videogames, tickle baby toes. It just takes a little bit of focus and intention.

My *tía* Silvia is exchanging snide remarks with my dad who has pushed his way into the kitchen for more food. They don't notice that I'm watching, leaning against the kitchen counter. She makes him wait for his food while he tries to get her to argue with him. My grandmother is sitting nearby and observing her grown children from the plastic lawn chair they've brought inside the house for her. Wrapped in a wool shawl, she clutches her rosary and prayer book. My *tía* begins to shout but catches herself and lowers her voice once again as my dad laughs at her. My grandmother begins to tremble and prays faster under her breath, shutting her eyes.

I notice my mother is looking at me, standing alone by the dinner table, waiting for me to come talk to her. I am relieved to see her. I tell my mom what is happening to me and the things that I have figured out I can do. Like talk and get others to see me.

"And now what, *mija*?" she asks, with a tired sigh. She holds my hand tightly.

"Just wait for the body to do what it needs to do."

"And then?"

"I don't know." She is silent.

"But you see, there's no reason to worry. Nothing can be more work or more strange than this," I tell her. My mother agrees, watching my father turn bright red, all taunting laughter gone, and my aunt pointing at his face with an accusatory spoon.

I DECIDE TO try walking my body. It turns out that it's something like riding a bike. Although riding a bike is different, since the bike was never an extension of me, as my legs once were. Now, however, my legs, arms, shoulders and head are not extensions of me, and my body is something I operate like a bike. I can do it almost naturally, without thinking too much about it.

I try walking my body into the house. The men continue talking about soccer, holding their freshly cracked cans of beer as they move out of the way for my body to pass. A small child runs into my leg. I am slightly nervous that when I walk my body into the house, my family and the other people who've been arriving will become alarmed. I walk into the crowded kitchen and one of my *tías* nudges me on the shoulder, squeezes a quick smile and says "Excuse me, *mija*" as she rushes out with a bowl of food. I know she knows I'm dead, but she doesn't seem to mind. The kitchen is more crowded now. I see women I don't know. My *tia* Silvia is showing them what's in the boiling pots. I realize I'm blocking the space with my less-than-coordinated body and shuffle into the living room, which is crowded now, too. Everyone is busy talking, laughing, eating and drinking. I think I hear other *tías* bickering somewhere. One of my cousins, Norma, says, "Excuse me, *prima*" as she reaches for a diaper bag I'm standing next to. A friend of another cousin coolly raises his chin at me to say, "Wussup."

My *tía* Martina has arrived with her partner Miriam. They are standing in the living room already arguing. Miriam looks very angry, questioning my *tía* Martina about a woman she was out with until very late last night. Miriam demands to know why she didn't come home right after work. She accuses my *tía* of cheating on her with this woman. My *tía* Martina doesn't want to talk about it now. She has only recently started attending family events and visiting relatives again after so many years. She doesn't want everyone to see this. They are suspicious of her enough as it is. My *tía* Martina tries telling Miriam that this is not the appropriate place or time to have this discussion. Miriam, as usual, does not seem to understand or care.

A few of my aunts offer to bring Miriam some food, some coffee, a chair, an aspirin. The kids on the couch look away from their videogame for a moment to see what the noise is about and turn back uninterested. The toddlers chew on their fingers, look up at the adults and scurry away from their big feet. My grandmother is sitting on her plastic lawn chair, watching and listening to all of this. Alone, she begins to weep softly, covering her face with one of her hands. The other hand in her lap holds the rosary and her prayer book.

A DEEP STIRRING in my body reminds me that I must make sure it decays properly. I walk my body to the bathroom. I walk down the hallway, crowded with older cousins carrying their new babies, and younger cousins who have moved their game of freeze tag indoors. The bathroom door is cracked open so I walk in. My cousin Alex is drying his hands with a towel by the sink.

"Oh, hey. I'm sorry, cousin," I say. "I just need to use the bathroom for a minute."

"Oh, yeah, go ahead," He finishes drying off his hands and pats me on the shoulder as he walks out and shuts the door behind him. I lock the door. Finally some quiet.

I lean against the bathroom counter and look into the mirror over the sink. I see a reflection of the upper half of my body. That is my face without expression. Those are my eyes sunken into dark circles. Those are my bluish lips. That is my skin in a color I can't describe.

I support myself by holding onto the counter as I lean over the sink. I see the black drain hole and my mouth opens. A steady gush of liquids streams out. I don't gag or heave and it doesn't hurt. I know what is happening. I just keep my mouth open wide enough so it all drops right into the drain. The liquids pour out in different colors, some white, some yellow, green, brown or orange, pink or even red. Sometimes clear. Some are more like mucus, some like mush, some like clumps or chunks, some just like water. As I wait for the stream to cease, I understand that the variations correspond to each of my body's organs.

When it's done, I rinse out my mouth and make sure the sink is clean. My body is significantly lighter, emptier without all those unnecessary fluids. I understand that this is just part of the process. I am confident it is going as it should.

I leave the bathroom and again look for my mother. I tell her about the vomit and she nods, standing very close to me, her

115

shoulder pressing against my arm. When I finish telling her, she fixes her eyes gently on my face, noting the changes. I see her too, her own face tired from waiting with me through the process. My face is a mirror of hers in the future, one day she will be here too. I sigh, and she kisses me on the cheek. We have always been strange mirrors for each other, my mother and I. Though she has not yet gone through this, she observes and learns what must be done.

THE HOUSE IS very crowded now. Among the crowd I see Indalesio, an uncle's distant relative, walking around with a plate full of food and talking with his mouth full. He has brought his entire family with him, his daughters Blanca, Susie and Jasmine, his sons Gabriel and Yeeyo. I haven't seen any of these people in years. They hardly ever spoke to me. I'm almost certain that the two oldest girls, Blanca and Susie, disliked me when I was alive, and Indalesio hardly knew I existed. I can tell Blanca and Susie didn't want to come in the first place and yet here they are, bitterly helping the older women chop onions and burning their fingers while they heat tortillas on the *comal*.

IT FEELS MUCH emptier in here now without all of the bodily fluids sloshing around, and I have to try a little harder to operate my body, to keep the spine upright, the arms and legs swinging just right to propel it forward, keep the flesh in a proper shape over my bones.

I really just need to lay my body back down. People can talk while I lie here on the cement by the avocado tree. But even listening to them is getting to be too much trouble. My attention is diffused, already a hovering layer of air. When I fix my eyes on the sky, I see an airplane trailing a long white arc, its tail already dispersing, erasing the memory of itself in its trajectory. Not long ago I would have looked for meaning in these etchings, imagined a symbol in a cloud, conjured a language. There is no time for symbols now, only the blunt truths of nature and its machines.

I'VE BEEN LYING here, alone, for a while now. I don't know how long, though the patio is nearly dark except for a single bulb. The men smoke and take shots of tequila by the door, closer to the kitchen. As the day has extinguished and evening's chill set in, hardly anyone has come out to look, except the strangers that are just arriving. They stand over me and look at my body stretched out on the cement. They walk back in without a thing to say.

I'm concentrating more now on the subtle but constant shifts taking place inside the walls of my body. The process is accelerating, I believe. I know there is something else that must be taken care of in order to carry on properly. So I rise, body and all, with some difficulty, and it takes great care to walk back inside. The house is practically impenetrable now, with so many people, most of whom I hardly remember or never even knew at all. The volume of so many conversations has escalated so that it's almost impossible to distinguish the voice of any single person. There are so many bodies around, I'm certain hardly anyone can recognize anyone else or hear what they are saying.

But somehow, my mother finds me amidst this mass of people and helps me move through it, holding me carefully by the arm.

"Mom, I need to go to the bathroom." I'm not sure if my mouth formed the words for her to hear, but she knows to lead me to the bathroom, parting a way for us through the bodies. She lets me go in alone and shuts the door.

The bathroom's quiet is a relief.

As I walk past the large mirror, from the corner of my eye, I glimpse a reflection of my body's bulk moving. I get the quick impression of nothing more than a self-animated frame draped in a material I know but don't actually recognize as my skin. There's hardly anything human about it.

As soon as I sit on the toilet all of my organs spill out in great slippery pulps. Out my intestines, out my stomach, my kidneys, my liver, my spleen, my lungs. Out my heart, out my brain. Out out out until I am purged clean, absolutely hollow and empty inside except for the bones that hold the whole thing up.

What a relief to be rid of all that. I feel more prepared now.

I AM STANDING at the edge of the crowd that has gathered to watch my *tía* Martina and her partner fight. A small bunch of toddlers watch my grandmother weep loudly in her chair. They suck their sticky thumbs with concern. My *tía* is holding Miriam by the wrists to keep her from beating her or harming herself, or breaking something in someone else's house. Miriam sobs and screams so no one can understand what she's saying. *"Miriam, por favor, cálmate,"* my *tía* tells her over and over, worried and embarrassed in front of her family, turning bright pink. Everyone is watching the two women struggle and scream. My grandmother slumps in her chair weeping, lamenting out loud. *"Ay dios mío"* she cries over and over. The youngest great grandchildren surround her and watch her wide-eyed and open-mouthed, candied drool dribbling over their pudgy fists and stained shirts. Miriam suddenly drops, and my *tía* has to quickly pull her up to keep her from hitting the tile floor. My *tía* accidentally bumps hard into a table behind her and knocks over a crystal vase that breaks in a loud crash. My grandmother lets out a long scream of anguish and horror, crying out *"¡Sálvanosi"* and falls from her chair in a soft thud. One of the babies begins to cry and everyone turns to see my grandmother lying still on the tile floor.

"LOOK, MAMI, HOW dry my hands are." The rest of my body too. The flesh is so dry now it hardly looks like flesh. My mother holds my hands very gently. We sit out on the stoop of the back door to the patio. The uncles have taken their tequila bottle inside the house. We are alone.

My body is now so brittle that I can no longer use it without parts of it falling off. I must leave it out on the cement patio to fall apart on its own.

"Mamá, will you help me?" She helps me up and we walk toward the avocado tree. She helps me lay my body on the ground and sits next to me. We are both waiting. If I wanted I

could step out of my body and go back into the house with my mother so she's not cold out here. My body would continue to blacken and dry out regardless. But I want to lie inside my body as it begins to cave in. My ribs break down into the cement, my legs and arms shake into thick dry flakes.

"*Mami*, everything is okay. I'm right here."

She can't hold me anymore. My lips and my mouth collapse, but I don't need them. We are waiting for everything to break up into dust and be carried away in the wind. This is turning out better than I expected.

ABOUT THE AUTHOR

~~~~~~

THE DAUGHTER OF Mexican immigrants, Carribean Fragoza was raised in South El Monte, California. After graduating from UCLA, Fragoza completed the Creative Writing MFA Program at CalArts, where she worked with writers Douglas Kearney and Norman Klein. Today, Fragoza co-edits UC Press's acclaimed California cultural journal, *Boom California*, and is also the founder of South El Monte Arts Posse, an interdisciplinary arts collective.

Her fiction and nonfiction have appeared numerous publications, including *BOMB, Huizache*, and the *Los Angeles Review of Books*. She is the co-editor of *East of East: The Making of Greater El Monte*, published February 2020 by Rutgers University Press, and Senior Writer at the *Tropics of Meta*. Carribean is the Coordinator of the Kingsley and Kate Tufts Poetry Award at Claremont Graduate University, and she lives in the San Gabriel Valley in LA County.

More at Carribean's website: http://carribeanfragoza.com/

ACKNOWLEDGMENTS

~~~~~

MY GREATEST GRATITUDE to the publications in which the following stories first appeared: "Lumberjack Mom" in *Huizache;* "Vicious Ladies" in *Bomb Magazine;* "Eat the Mouth That Feeds You" in *Nat.Brut;* "Crystal Palace" in *Air/Light;* and "Ini y Fati" in *Zzyzzyva.*

Shout outs to the El Monte and South El Monte writers who did it before me: Salvador Plascencia, Michael Jaime-Becerra and Toni Margarita Plummer. My thanks to the Mountain View School District and whoever ran the Young Writers' Tea from 1989-1994. Dana Johnson and Alex Espinoza, your portraits of the San Gabriel Valley are among my treasures.

Humble and deep bows to all the homies who created and held space, offered a spark from which to build a fire: Laura Vena, Janice Lee, Harold Abramowitz, Amanda Ackerman, Jen Hofer, Vincent Ramos, Xochitl-Julissa Bermejo, Las Guayabas comprised of Estela Gonzales, Tatiana de la Tierra, Myriam Gurba, and Griselda Suarez. Fresno writers, thank you for making Fresno a home. The wise guidance of Bruce Bauman during my time at CalArts and the Chicana writing workshop with Alicia Gaspar de Alba at UCLA have been invaluable in this journey.

Vickie Vértiz, gracias for being a light, seeing it when I couldn't. Your friendship has been sage and salve. My best Chicanita, Maria Lucero Ortiz, from one coast to the other, to the ruins of Chichen Itza and back again, gracias por tu apoyo. Janet Sarbanes, mi hada madrina, thank you for your confidence and encouragement throughout the years. Sesshu Foster and Ben Ehrenreich, this book would not have been possible without your collective generosity.

My thanks to the Guzmán family for all your kindness and patience. Thank you to my daughters, Aura and Camila for sharing your mother with this thing called writing. Romeo, my relentless muse, I owe you everything. My siblings, Chris and Jamie, and my father, Jaime, are in my heart in all I do. I am most graciously indebted to my mother, Ceci, my grandmother Cecilia, and my great-grandmother Chuy, for the lessons and the love. All flowers and copalli to the ancestors and our vicious goddesses for the fangs.